CITY
OF THE
LOST

CITY
OF THE
LOST

DAW BOOKS, INC.

DONALD A. WOLLHEIM, FOUNDER

375 Hudson Street, New York, NY 10014

ELIZABETH R. WOLLHEIM

SHEILA E. GILBERT

PUBLISHERS

http://www.dawbooks.com

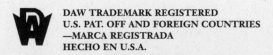

CITY

OF THE

LOST

Chapter 1

I toss my jacket on the bar, slide onto the red vinyl stool next to Julio. He's on his sixth drink of the day, and it's not even noon. Empty shotglasses lie scattered on the bar. Julio's a tequila man, likes Patrón when he can get it, Cuervo when he can't. Me, I'm a scotch drinker. I order a Johnny Walker Black, neat.

"The fuck you doin' here, Joe?" he says, taking a sidelong glance at me through unfocused eyes. Besides the bartender, we're the only ones here. Henry's Bar and Grill on Magnolia isn't the worst in town, but it's as bad as you'll find in North Hollywood. Everything's done up in faux red leather and brass tacks. Looks like Hell if Satan were a lounge singer. Julio's a regular. If he isn't out working with me or at home with his wife, Mariel, he's in here tossing back a few.

"I was about to ask you the same thing," I say. "You were supposed to be at Simon's last night. You talk to the Italian? You get the stone?"

Simon Patterson's our boss. Crazy English fucker hired us to break legs, shove hands down garbage disposals. The rest of the body, too, if need be. We're good at our jobs. He pays us well.

"Yeah," he says. "I talked to him."

"And the stone? You got it?"

He shakes his head. Great. No stone, and he's too fucking drunk to think straight. He gets a thousand-yard stare. After a moment he looks up at me, a plea in his eyes. "I can't do it, man."

"Do what?"

He shakes his head. "This," he says, staring at his hands and arms. He grabs me by the collar, pulls me close. "This is forever, man. This is fucking forever. I can't do forever. I can't fucking do it."

Okay, time to not poke the crazy bear. I ease his hands off me. I look him over. He's a mess. Bloodshot eyes. Hands shaking. Hasn't slept. More skittish than I've ever seen him. He's freaked the fuck out, and that scares the shit out of me.

Julio's the biggest Filipino I know. Six two. As bad-ass as they come. Benches three-fifty, dragon tattoos on his shoulders. Beats the crap out of Samoans for fun. Made the mistake of going a couple rounds with him at the gym, and he laid me out with a concussion and a missing tooth. If Julio's scared, there's got to be one hell of a good reason for it.

Last night Simon told him to lean on Sandro Giavetti, Italian guy from Chicago. Hit the wop at his hotel.

"Jesus, man. The fuck happened to you?" I say to Julio.

Week ago, Giavetti comes to Simon looking to buy things that don't get bought. Has a job to hit a house and get some gemstone.

Anyway, Simon hooks him up with three boys good at B&E and gets a nice fat cut for being a middleman. Thing is, two of them have gone missing, third one's dead. Blew his brains out night before last. Word is they found a clip's worth of shell casings, but only one bullet, the one he used to paint his wall.

Normally Simon wouldn't give a fuck. But then the rumors started up that Simon had something to do with whatever the hell went down. Guy like Simon, he works on reputation. Worth more than gold. He figures Giavetti spread the word around, and now Simon's got to show him that that shit doesn't fly.

Julio pours himself another shot, tosses it back like it's mother's milk. Stares at his hands. "Look what he did to me."

I crane my head to look at his hands. I don't see what the big deal is. "They look fine, Julio."

"No, man. They're not. They're not my hands. They're his. They're his fucking hands."

I smack him on the back of his head. "Hey. Snap the fuck out of it."

So Simon sends Julio over to Giavetti's hotel. Take the old fucker out, walk off with the stone. Fuck knows what Simon wants with it. Principal of the thing, I suppose. Whatever. Point is that Julio was supposed to report back last night and never showed.

My phone chirps at me from my jacket pocket. It's Simon. "Joe, me old china," he says, Cockney coming through like he hasn't spent fifteen years stateside. "You found him?"

"Yeah," I say. "He's freaking out. Something happened, but he hasn't told me what yet."

"He look all right?"

"He looks like shit," I say. "I don't think he's slept. Drinking early, too." In fact, he looks worse than he did a minute ago. I do a double take. Yeah, like his face has started to sink in on itself or something.

Julio closes his eyes, folds his hands together. Starts muttering in Tagalog.

"Talked to Giavetti, ain't he?"

"Yeah, he's talked to him. Least I think so. He's acting kinda weird." Simon's voice, urgent now. "He got the stone?"

I glance over at Julio. Christ, I think he's praying. "No," I say. "Says he didn't get it. Look, I think I need to get him outta here." The bartender's giving us the stink eye, and if Julio goes bugfuck better he do it in private.

"I need that stone, Joe. I fucking need it, mate. Find out where it is. If he saw Giavetti, he saw the stone. He knows where it is." Simon's voice, breathless, high-pitched.

"Jesus, calm down," I say. "I'll find out." Simon can be a real asshole sometimes.

"Julio," I say. "Simon wants to—-" I jump at the sound of shattering glass. Julio's grabbed his bottle of Cuervo and smashed it against the bar.

My instinct is to get away, though I can't believe he'd come at me with it. I roll out of his way anyway, torque my left knee in the process.

Turns out I'm not the guy who needs to worry.

Julio grabs the bartender by the shirt, pulls him in, takes a good, long swipe with the bottle. The guy screams, flailing to get away.

Julio drags the bartender closer, his jaws snapping. Like he wants to rip through the guy's sternum and chow down on him.

I ignore the pain in my knee and jump at Julio. Hook him in a full nelson and pull him away. Nobody's fool, the bartender bolts for the back room.

"The fuck are you doing, man?" I yell. Julio's only answer is to grunt and spit and wave that goddamn busted tequila bottle around.

I try to angle him so I can get him on the floor, but before I can get any real purchase he heaves forward and throws me clear over the bar. I slam into a wall of Wild Turkey and Maker's Mark, glass shattering around me.

I hit the floor on my torn knee, cut myself on shards of glass. On the other side of the bar Julio's pacing like a panther on heroin, swinging the bottle. Muttering and growling. Julio's completely fucking lost it. The hell is he on?

I grab a paring knife behind the bar. It's only got a three-inch blade but it's better than nothing. I limp out from behind the bar, grab a stool, keep my distance.

He whirls around, sees me. His muttering turns into a scream and he charges, waving the broken bottle around less like a weapon and more like he just can't think of anything else to do with it.

Barstool in one hand, paring knife in the other, I feel like a retarded lion tamer.

And just as he's about to slam into me he stops.

The look in his eyes changes to something I've never seen before. Pleading, praying. For a split second Julio's back. Long enough, it seems, to say good-bye.

He shoves the splintered bottle into his throat, tears a ragged gash from Adam's apple to jugular, angles it up, and cranks it deep through the back of his throat.

Blood erupts like oil from a derrick. I drop the knife and barstool, frantic. Try to stop the bleeding. I can hear Simon's tinny voice from my phone on the floor saying, "What? What?" over and over again. I grab bar towels, my jacket, anything that can staunch the blood.

None of it matters. Julio's eyes roll up into the back of his head. His life bubbles red down the front of his shirt.

———

Frank Tanaka is smoking at me.

He's on his third Kool since sitting down across from me in one of the interrogation rooms at the North Hollywood police station on Burbank Boulevard. They did a crappy job with the soundproofing and I can hear the traffic on the 170 Freeway a block away.

I look over at the NO SMOKING sign plastered on the wall. Frank catches my gaze. Blows smoke in my face.

"Suppose you want one," he says. I do, but we both know he won't give me one, and I wouldn't take it anyway.

"Menthols are for pussies."

Frank Tanaka's one of those little Japanese guys martial arts students get warned about. He's small and wiry and I have no doubt he can kick my ass, however much he smokes.

He presses a button on the small recorder sitting between us, tells it the date and time.

"So, Sunday, why'd you kill Julio?"

"Talk to the bartender," I say for the fifth or sixth time. "He'll tell you the same thing. Julio killed himself." By the time the cops got their act together enough to talk to me, it was already four in the afternoon. I've managed to clean up a little, but there's a stickiness on my hands that won't come off no matter how many times I scrub. My shirt's caked with Julio's blood, and my knee's swollen from where I twisted it at the bar. The damn thing throbs if I look at it funny, ever since I tore it wrestling in high school. These bastards could have given me some Advil.

At least they gave me Band-Aids for the glass cuts on my hands.

"Don't bullshit me, Sunday." Frank glares at me, the sleeves of his salmon oxford rolled up to his elbows, his Mr. Miyagi mustache twitching. "Julio Guerrera's not the kind of guy to kill himself."

He's got me there. Four hours ago I would have agreed with him. Hell, I agree with him now. Julio and suicide are not two things that go together.

"I dunno. Couldn't cover his bets, maybe?"

Frank knows I'm holding something back. He knew Julio almost as well as I did. God knows he's arrested both of us enough times: suspicion of murder, aggravated assault. Tried to grab me on jaywalking once just to get me in the station. He's never had enough to make anything stick though.

We go back and forth like this a couple more rounds, as if he thinks repetition's going to get me to change my story. Then he drops a grenade into the conversation.

"So what's the deal with Sandro Giavetti?" I almost jump when he says it, but I've been in rooms like this since I was selling pot down in Venice twenty years ago, and I'm not about to slip now.

"Sandra? Never heard of her," I say. "Julio's wife's gonna be pissed."

"I know Julio was with Giavetti last night."

"Don't know who you're talking about." Frank shuts up and does The Stare. Every cop's got one. Look hard, say nothing. Most folks will spill their guts just to fill the void and get the conversation going again. I'm not that easy. He's been using The Stare on me for years.

A minute later there's a knock, and a uniform sticks her head around the door. "Counsel's here to see him," she says. Frank and her glare at each other with a look that screams bad breakup. Lucky me. She ushers one of Simon's faceless lawyers into the room before Frank can so much as open his mouth.

The man's got on a gray Armani suit, conspicuous Rolex. His haircut probably cost as much as my shoes. "Detective," he says. He gives Frank a look like a nun catching a boy in the girls' bathroom. "Good to see you again."

"Counselor," Frank says. He knows he's got nothing on me. This interview's over. He stands, pulls a business card from his pocket, scribbles a number on the back, and hands it to me.

"You see anything weird. Anything. Call me." He walks out the door. Slams it behind him.

"You certainly know how to make friends, don't you, Mr. Sunday?" the attorney asks. He sits down in front of me, places his calfskin briefcase on the table, pops it open. "Sorry to hear about your associate," he says with as much emotion as if he's ordering a sandwich.

"Yeah," I say. "It sucked."

Of everything that's happened today, Frank giving me his card spins me the most. Arrest me one minute, give me his phone number the next. Reminds me of a bad date. I stick it in my jacket pocket just to get it out of my sight.

"Did you kill him?"

"Christ, not you, too."

He holds his hands out, placating. "Just have to ask," he says. "I take it that's a no, then. The bartender gave the same story, after he was sedated enough to stop screaming. Seems to think Mr. Guerrero was trying to eat him or something. We should have you out in no time, considering that you haven't been formally charged with anything."

"How long is 'no time'?" I ask.

He looks behind him at the door. "From here on out it's just paperwork. But it'll be easier if we sit here a few minutes. The detective's pretty pissed."

Chapter 2

Simon's got a house north of the Palisades overlooking the ocean and Pacific Coast Highway. The sound of the waves mix with the traffic, a low-grade static that drowns out the noises in my head.

He's called a meeting here, a place he uses for entertaining D-list Hollywood celebs, producers, the occasional fresh-faced ingénue. He's behind a lot of money in L.A., though he doesn't advertise it. You won't see his name in *Variety*, and he likes it that way.

Of course, he's late, but since he's the boss that means I'm early. I let myself in with a spare key and an alarm code. Julio and I used this place occasionally to regroup after a job, so we always had a key.

Christ. It's hard to think of Julio in the past tense. I'd headed home after they released me, iced my knee, rebandaged the worst of the cuts. Cleaned myself up. Spent the whole time wondering what I was going to tell Julio's wife.

Don't know if the cops will do it, but I know Simon won't. She'll be taken care of, though. Simon's got this thing about loyalty. Once you're in, you're in. But no way is he going to talk to her. That's going to be my job, like it or not.

She won't take it well. Julio never told her what he did for a living. She thinks he's a manager for a construction company in Hollywood. Julio met her back in Manila where she grew up thinking she couldn't do anything by herself. Still thinks she needs a man around to make things happen. Surprised she gets out of bed when he's not around.

Julio told me once that she made him feel necessary. Special. I told him it was fucked up.

I called her on the way over to Simon's. Got the answering machine. Julio's gravelly voice told me to leave a message, so I did. Started to say that Julio killed himself, but it felt weird telling a dead man's voice what it should already know. Told Mariel to call me later.

I'm on my fourth Marlboro and third Tecate when the front door opens. Simon I'm expecting, but Danny's a surprise.

Danny Harrison is Simon's—hell I don't know what to call him. Administrative assistant? Foreman? Operational manager?

Bald guy, slick talker. Lots of tattoos. Always wears this goddamn porkpie hat makes him look like an extra in *Swingers*.

Simon owns a club in Hollywood where he does most of his business. Shakes up the theme of the place every couple nights. Fetish crowd one night, swing dancers another, headbangers when he can squeeze them in. Simon likes to diversify.

Danny runs the club and handles some of the less-than-legal business dealings. A real up-and-comer that Danny. I hear Simon lets him run some prostitution out of there as a sideline.

The times I usually deal with him directly are when I'm picking up a clean gun or Julio and I pull bodyguard duty for Simon at the club.

"Joseph," Simon says, coming out onto the deck with Danny in tow. "Wasn't sure if you were going to make it. Danny, get the man a drink." I raise my beer, and he nods. "Then get me a drink."

Simon's built like a fireplug, squat and solid, but a good twenty years older than he looks. Thinning hair. Likes boiled British food a little too much for his doctor's comfort, but he doesn't care. Man's got so much money he's immortal. He can afford to live large.

He claps a thick hand on my shoulder. "You all right, lad?"

"Yeah," I say. "Just been a long day."

He hangs his head, nods. "It has been at that," he says, peers up at me. "Going to be longer still. This isn't over yet, Joe."

"What's not over, Simon?" Something in me threatens to snap. I don't get angry. It's unprofessional, gives the other guy an advantage. I force myself to relax as best I can, but it leaks out the edges, anyway.

"Do you know why he did this?" I step in closer, show him my hands. Julio's blood still under my fingernails. "He tore his own fucking throat out."

Simon steps back slowly, and it's then I realize he's got a blade milli-meters from spilling my intestines to the floor. It's easy to forget how fast he is with a knife.

"Calm yourself, Joseph. That's what we're here to discuss, innit?" He looks around, peering into the hazy shade of blue that passes for a dark night in Los Angeles. "But not out here." He heads back into the living room. I hang back a moment to pull myself together, then follow him in.

He slides the door closed. Locks it. Draws the curtains. "I don't know if that'll help," he says, more to himself than to us. Danny hands him a scotch and soda. He tosses it back like water, throws himself into one of the leather Manhattan chairs.

"Give us a rundown on what happened," Simon says.

I give them the details. But when I get to the part about Julio going to retrieve the stone Simon gives me a shut-the-fuck-up look, and I bounce past that detail.

Danny doesn't seem to notice the omission. I wonder if Simon's told him about it. And wonder why he wouldn't.

"Giavetti killed Julio," he says. Holds up a hand when I open my mouth. "Let me finish. Please. I don't know how, but I know he did it. Me and him, we go back quite a ways. When he came in to see me I nearly shat myself. I'm sixty-four now. Met Giavetti when I was eighteen. He looked just as old then as he does now. You following me?" He pauses to let it sink in. It doesn't.

"I saw the guy when he first came to see you," Danny says. "He's got to be in his eighties."

"I said the same thing back in 1959," says Simon.

"You sure it's the same guy?" I ask.

He laughs. "Oh, yes," he says. "Man like Giavetti, you never forget. Did odd jobs for him. Had his hands in a couple of brothels in London, horse racing, poker clubs."

He pauses, takes a deep breath. "Bloody queer thing. Spent a lot of time at libraries.

"One night," he says, "pal of mine gets the bright idea to bump him off. We'd been drinking, and we both knew Giavetti was loaded. So we figure we'll hide in a closet, strangle him in his sleep. My job was to get him in the house. I've got keys, I know when the ol' bugger goes to bed."

"You tried to kill him?" Danny asks.

"Not tried. Tied him up good, beat him to death with a cricket bat. Let him bleed out on his Persian rugs and laughed the whole time. Stuffed our pockets with as much as we could carry. Set the place alight. He was dead, all right. I watched him burn."

I look over at Danny to see if he's buying any of this.

"Bullshit," he says.

"I'm with Danny on this one," I say. "You're saying Giavetti's ghost is back, and he somehow got Julio to kill himself? Come on, Simon. Don't lose it now. You killed Giavetti, what, almost fifty years ago? It's somebody else. What about your partner?"

"Lost his nerve," he says. "Talked about going to the police." Knowing Simon that means he's at the bottom of the Thames. Scratch that lead.

"Who else knew?"

"Besides you two, I've never told a soul. Back then Giavetti had connections. Word got out we'd done the deed, we were good as dead. No one else knew."

"Well, somebody knew and they're screwing with you. And I'm betting the guys you brokered to steal this stone were in on it. Have to be. The dead one lost his nerve, the others took him out."

"The missing bullets?"

"Vests," Danny says, getting into it. "The bullets are stuck in their Kevlar." Starting to make sense, pieces all lining up. Simon's nodding slowly at the scenario.

"Then why'd Julio kill himself after meeting him?" he says.

"Okay, enough," Danny says. "This is a nice chat around the campfire telling ghost stories and all. Maybe later we can roast s'mores and sing 'Kumbaya.' But right now you've got some fucker impersonating a guy you killed fifty years ago. It's that or you're going senile, and I'm betting that ain't your problem."

"So you think this is just a trick, then?"

"I'll admit it's a weird angle to play," I say. "But yeah. He's got a point."

When Simon grabs onto an idea he doesn't let go of it. Most stubborn man I've ever met. He's got that tone that says we're in for a long night of arguing.

He thinks for a long moment. "You're right," he says finally.

"Come again?"

"I said, you're right. Has to be an impersonator. The man's dead. Years now."

Something's wrong. Simon never gives up a point this easily. What the hell is he playing at?

"Danny's got a point. It doesn't matter," Simon says. He nods at Danny, who gets up to fix him another scotch and soda. "Somebody's fucking with me. I want him gone."

"Hallelujah," Danny says. "He sees the light."

Simon gives Danny a cold smile. I don't think Simon's going to quickly forget that senile crack.

"When?" I ask.

"Tonight," Simon says. He raises his empty glass. "Danny, would you get me another?" Deflated at being his serving boy, Danny goes to freshen his drink.

Simon opens a drawer in the table next to his chair, pulls out a Glock 30 with a threaded barrel and a silencer.

"Use this," he says, handing them to me. "They're clean."

Danny comes back with a new glass. Simon slams it back. "I'm heading out of town," he says. "Going to San Diego for a couple of days. Bit of a holiday. Maybe do some fishing." The calm Simon shows the world is cracking. He doesn't drink this much, doesn't sweat this much.

"You're all I've got left, Joseph. I'm depending on you to escort our false Mr. Giavetti out of town before I get back. It's vital you do this. Probably the most important thing I've ever asked you to do."

He doesn't have to tell me to get the stone. That much is implied. An old man in a hotel room. Doesn't get any easier than that.

But why is it so goddamn important?

Chapter 3

It's just Danny and me standing in the gravel driveway, smoking. We watch as Simon drives off in his black Jag.

"What was that you two were talking about?" Danny asks.

"Giavetti. You were there. You going deaf or just senile?"

Danny laughs. "Speaking of which, he's gone round the bend, hasn't he?"

I shrug. "Maybe." I've been thinking since the phone call at the bar that Simon isn't acting quite right. Not quite Simon. Nothing gets to him, normally. He's fucking unflappable. His insistence on getting the rock just doesn't make sense. And now, with this story of Giavetti—

"What, you believe him?"

"Does it matter?" Sure, I got doubts, but I work for the man. Worked for him damn near twenty years. If he's going off the reservation, I'm going right there with him.

Danny thinks about what I've just said. "Guess not." The rear lights of the Jag disappear down a turn.

"Besides," I say, "if he really believed this was the same guy do you think he'd be sending me to kill him? Come on. Listen to him tell it, this guy's immortal."

"You want to look at it that way, sure. I still think he's off his nut." Danny takes a drag on his cig, blows out a lungful of smoke.

"My dad went senile," he says. "We had to stick him in a home. He couldn't remember who anybody was, shit himself every day. You ever have to deal with that kind of thing?"

"Never met my dad."

"That's gotta suck."

"Is this going somewhere?"

"Simon's not gonna live forever. Eventually, he'll do something stupid, and the whole thing's gonna come crashing round his ears. What then?"

"This a hypothetical?"

"What? Oh, calm down. I'm not trying to fuck him over. He's as much my meal ticket as he is yours. I'm just wondering what happens when he finally screws up. Or gets old and kicks. The man's sixty-five, for chrissake."

I toss my cigarette, grind it out with a heel. He's right. Simon is getting old. He's got no kids, no family I've ever heard of. What happens when he finally goes? It's not like I'm getting a pension off him.

"Simon's not senile."

"No, he was just telling us some dead mob boss from the fifties has come back from the grave to drive Julio crazy enough to commit suicide. I mean, I'm not saying Julio was exactly stable, but— What? Don't look at me like that. You're crazy, too."

"I just do what I'm told."

"Yeah," he says. "You just do what you're told. You're just a useful tool, right? See, that's the difference between you and me. You like taking orders. It frees you up from the heavy thinking."

I light a fresh Marlboro, blow smoke into the chill air. From where I'm standing I can just barely see a sliver of the ocean down across the lights of PCH.

"I ever tell you I don't like you much?" I ask.

"Good thing we're both professionals, then, huh?"

I've got a good fifty pounds on Danny. I could make him eat the sidewalk without breaking a sweat. But that'd just piss off Simon. Might be worth it, though.

Danny gets this worried look on his face when I don't say anything. Like he knows what I'm thinking. I don't want to be around this sonofabitch any more than I need to, so I drop the half finished cigarette, crush it into the pavement, head to my car.

"Hey," he says as I get in. "That senile crack? I was just joking. Don't need to tell Simon that. Right?"

I smile at him, say nothing, and pull out of the driveway. Let him chew on that for a while.

I don't give a fuck about what he says about Simon. He's probably right. The thing that's bothering me is what he said about Julio. About me.

Of course Julio was a little bit crazy. You can't stick a guy in a trunk and run him through a junkyard compactor if you're not a little bit off.

But Julio wasn't the kind of crazy that kills himself. Suicide's something you do to other people.

And what the fuck was that about being a useful tool? Fuck him. I'm not the one fetching Simon's drinks. The fuck does Danny think he is? I've never liked the guy, now I know why.

Sure, what I do is easier. Follow orders. Do what you're told. But I'm not a goddamn robot. I do this because I'm good at it. I like the work. I can handle anything that gets thrown at me.

But then, so could Julio.

I push the thought aside, head up PCH with the windows down. Cold air blows in the smell of the ocean. My knee aches past the Advil, so I chew up a couple more and swallow them dry. My stomach will pay for it later.

I call Giavetti's hotel on my cell, confirm he's still checked in. I'll have this sewn up before morning. Head over the hill to Du-par's for pancakes after.

I hang a right on Topanga, begin the long, curvy wind through the canyon to the 101. My cell phone chirps. I fumble it out of my jacket. It's Mariel, Julio's wife. Like I need this right now.

"Yeah."

"I just got home," Mariel says. "You called."

"Have the police called you yet?"

"Police?" she asks, wariness creeping into her voice. "Is Julio with you?"

"No," I say, not sure how to proceed. "He . . . look, Mariel, are you gonna be up for a while? I think I should come over."

A considering silence. "What's happened to Julio?"

How do you tell someone that her husband ripped through his own throat with a broken bottle?

There's a noise on the other end. "Hang on," she says, puts the phone down. A few seconds go by. "God, Joe, you had me scared there."

"Sorry?" I say.

"Julio," she says. "He just walked in. You want to talk to him?" Her voice fades in and out as I drive through a dead patch around Fernwood and start to lose the signal. "Honey," she says away from the mouthpiece, "Joe's on the phone."

"Mariel," I say. "Listen to me. Julio's not there. He's not coming home."

"No," she says. "He's right here. He's—" A pause.

And then she starts screaming.

"Mariel? What's happening?" If she answers me it's lost in a burst of digital static. The signal cuts out completely. I throw the phone into the passenger seat, stomp on the gas, and tear through the canyon as fast as my car will take me.

I cut the lights half a block from the house, park behind a pickup across the street. Did Mariel just snap? I never got she was all that stable to begin with. Or is there somebody actually in there? And if so, who is it?

One way to find out. I pull the pistol from under my seat and fit the suppressor over the barrel. Check the chamber, load a clip, rack the slide.

Front door's cracked open. I can see Mariel sitting on the floor at the foot of the sofa. I ease the door open, step inside.

And there's Julio sitting on the couch, Mariel's hand in his, head moving from side to side. He's got wide eyes, like he can't remember how to blink, a ragged flap of snake belly white skin and muscle where his throat used to be.

His mouth is working like a grouper, trying to make a sound, but nothing's coming out, not even a wheeze. Takes me a second to realize it's because he's not breathing.

Mariel turns to me when I come in, tears streaming down her face, mascara painting dark lines down to her chin. "Help him," she says to me. "Oh, God, please help him."

"Holy fuck," I say, my voice barely a whisper. I stand stock still, gun tight in my fist. I have no idea what to do. Seems a little late for the paramedics. I step slowly toward them, Julio barely acknowledging me, and touch him. His skin is clammy. I check his pulse. Nothing.

I remember Frank Tanaka's weirdly intense interest in Giavetti, the detective telling me to call him if I see anything weird. This is definitely fucking weird. But I bring him into this and Simon's fucked. Maybe me, too.

Julio turns to me, head lolling to one side. Yellow pus oozes out the gash in his throat.

To hell with Simon. All bets are off. This is the weirdest goddamn thing I've ever seen.

I dig around in my jacket for Frank's card. My phone is still in the car, so I grab Mariel's.

She's obsessively patting Julio's hand, rocking back and forth, saying, "It's okay, baby. It's all gonna be okay." Trying to hold things together, but she doesn't know how. I'm not sure I'm doing any better.

"I heard him come in," she says, her eyes glued to her husband. "And then I saw him like this. What happened to him, Joe?" Her body heaves with fresh sobs. "I don't know what to do."

The phone rings once, twice, then clicks as Frank comes on the line. "Hello?" he says, voice groggy with sleep.

"Frank," I say. "Joe Sunday. Look. Julio. . . ." I'm not sure what to say. I've got a dead man on the sofa, and I need some help. I think Giavetti might have something to do with it, and oh, by the way, my boss thinks he murdered him in London fifty years ago. And did I mention that the dead guy on the couch is still moving around?

What the hell am I doing, calling a goddamn cop?

"What?" he asks.

I take a deep breath. I need somebody who can think straight. Right now he's the only one who comes to mind. "It's Julio," I say. "He's—" There's a loud click. I think he's hung up on me, until I realize I'm not getting a dial tone.

"You can put the phone down," says a grainy voice, accent like Chicago. Chicago and something else I can't place. "It doesn't work, anyway."

Guy steps out from the kitchen. Tall. Wrinkled and balding. Liver spots on his hands and face.

"You've gotta be fucking kidding me." The man's old enough to be my great grandfather, but his hands and neck are all wiry muscle, and he's standing straight as a marine. Just like the security camera pic Simon showed me. I almost laugh but stop myself.

He may be old, but that Beretta in his hand isn't. I do what he says, put the phone back in its cradle.

"And the gun, too, if you don't mind."

"I think I'd rather not, thanks." God, but don't I just love a Mexican standoff.

"Joe, who is this?" Mariel asks. Giavetti smiles at her.

"Sandro Giavetti," he says. He grins at some inside joke. "You could say your husband and I are close."

She stands up. Steps into my line of fire before I can stop her. "Can you help him? He came home like this. I don't know what to do."

Giavetti moves to the side, each of us keeping our guns on the other. He shakes his head. "No. I was hoping this time would be different." Mariel looks even more lost than before.

"You did this to him," I say, more statement than question. It dawns on me that maybe Julio isn't the only one. "Who else? The two guys who stole for you? You tried to get the other one, but he killed himself before you got to him, didn't he?"

"I'm not having this conversation. I only want my property."

I look back at the mess on the couch that used to be Julio, gasping for air that never comes. His property?

"No. You're not taking him anywhere," I say.

Giavetti heaves a theatrical sigh. "Is this where you say something like 'over my dead body'?" he says. "Because we can do that."

"And what, we kill each other? You shoot me, I shoot you?"

He thinks about this. "You're right," he says. "Julio, kill him."

Julio lurches off the couch with inhuman speed. I spin around. I double tap two bloodless holes in his chest. The suppressor drops the sound to something like a loud slap. He doesn't even slow down.

Mariel screams. Runs to him. He backhands her with the force of a bulldozer. She hits the wall like a sack of garbage, bones cracking like glass.

Takes me a second to realize I've got my priorities screwed up. I turn to take out Giavetti, but he's already on me. Old man moves like a goddamn ninja. Sweeps the gun from me with one hand. I take a jab with my left, and he ducks under it like he's twenty years old.

He delivers a side kick to my bad knee. Tendons shred, the kneecap pops over to the side. I drop in a wave of agony, punching out and clocking him on the side of the face, but by then Julio's got me by the throat.

He lifts me off the floor. Shakes me, a dog with a gopher. I've got no air. Punches are useless. I snag the skin flap at his throat and tear a meaty chunk off, but it doesn't faze him. He's crushing my windpipe, and I can't make him let go.

My lungs are screaming. I can feel my eyes bugging out, blood so tight in my head my face is burning. My entire chest is on fire. I get tunnel vision, shades of gray fading in from the edges. Nothing left but empty gasping as my body tries to get some oxygen.

A thousand miles away, I can hear Giavetti's laughter.

Chapter 4

When the water hits me, it takes a second to remember I'm not in jail.

Back in the nineties I spent three months sitting in county on a weapons beef that ended in a hung jury. Green-gray industrial paint, grimy white tile. When I open my eyes, it's like having flashbacks.

"Mornin', sunshine." Giavetti tosses the empty bucket as I splutter water out of my mouth.

Hands cuffed above my head to a broken shower tap jutting out of the tiled wall. Dirty water dripping from busted ceiling pipes swirls down rusted drains. A single light hangs from the ceiling, throwing out a flickering pool of yellow.

The walls are covered in gang signs, the floor in broken bottles and crack vials. Stink in the air like meat gone too long in an unplugged fridge.

Last thing I remember is Julio crushing my windpipe, squeezing me like an overripe tomato. Breathing feels funny, air not coming in quite right. Something wrong with the sound in the room. Quiet in a way I can't place. Something missing.

I run through my catalog of injuries, and they're all coming up blank. Throat, knee, all those old aches and pains that I'd learned to ignore are gone, conspicuous in their absence. The fuck is wrong with me?

I tug on the cuffs, more to give me something else to think about than from any realistic hope of getting out.

"Sorry, son. Police issue. They're not coming off."

Giavetti crouches, far enough away that I can't get to him, jaundiced in the dim light. He's got a blue polo shirt, chinos, pair of slip-on loafers. If not for the Beretta in his hand and the gleam of insanity in his eye, he'd look a lot like my grandfather.

"How are you feeling? Wondering when you were going to come back."

"Fuck you." I give the cuffs another tug. Like I could be anywhere else.

"Now there's a pity. I was hoping for better than that. Fact you can talk at all's a good sign, though. Let's try something else. What's Simon's problem?"

I give him the finger, just in case he didn't catch me the first time around.

"Interesting. That's different. That's good. What if I said please?"

I stare at him for a good long minute, and with each passing second he's getting happier and happier. I finally open my mouth just to burst his bubble.

"Simon didn't send Julio to kill you. Just wanted to talk. Find out if you knew what happened to the guys you hired from him."

"Just talk," he says. "Right. So he sends his goddamn gorilla over with an ax handle? Just like London." He twists his mouth and a pretty good impersonation of Simon comes out. "'No 'ard feelins. Bygones 'n all that.' Limey cocksucker. They're dead. He knows why. And what about you? Suppose I'd be seeing you for a 'talk' sometime? No, not a goddamn thing's changed."

"The fuck do you want, anyway?"

The question seems to surprise him. "You're always this inquisitive, aren't you? That's really good." He pulls up a half-burned sofa cushion and sits back on it. "I want to be left the fuck alone. I want Simon to hold up his end of the bargain and not try to rip me off again."

"The man's got people lining up to suck his dick. What the hell could he possibly want from you?" The longer I stall him, the better chance I have of getting out of this mess.

Giavetti belts out a laugh like a mule. "Oh. You poor, dumb bastard. You've no idea what this is about, do you?"

He settles in on the cushion, cross-legged. Like he's about to tell stories to the third graders.

"Immortality," he says. "Living forever. It's a neat trick, if you can pull it off."

If I hadn't already known I was being held by a psychopath this pretty much clinches it. Play along, Sunday. Stall for time. Talk slow to the crazy guy with the gun and maybe you'll walk out of here. Oh, and ignore that whole zombie Julio problem that's banging on the back of your skull.

"Suppose you can do it, huh?"

"Of course I can. And Simon knows it. That's why you're here. Betting he fed you a load of horseshit, but trust me, that's the reason."

"Is it now? And here's me thinking I was coming to feed you to a woodchipper."

"The thing that gets me," he says, ignoring me, "is how he's able to get you stupid fuckers to listen to him. I mean, he is one of the worst liars I've ever met. What is it? Is it that you want to believe him? Is that it? Or does he just make his bullshit sound better than the truth?"

"Hear him tell it, he handed your ass to you in London."

Giavetti's eyes flash, the grandfatherly mask twisting into something darker, older. Like he's got a demon under his skin, and he's barely keeping it inside. I almost start to believe that Simon was right.

Just as quickly it's gone. The grin is back on his face. Like it never left.

"Yeah, well, there is that," he says with a shrug. "I got lazy. Get to be my age, and it's a wonder you can remember where your own dick is. I owe him for London. He thought he took me out. But, hey, I'm a survivor. Little this, little that. I'm good as new."

"Fountain of Youth, right? Live forever?"

"Exactly."

I nod at his sallow arms, skin hanging off the bone like a liquefied chicken. "Didn't stick, did it?"

"Well, maybe not Fountain of Youth so much as Fountain of Not Staying Dead. But I'm working on that one." He rummages around in his pocket. "Hey, want to see something neat?"

He pulls out a stone, an opal about the size of a small egg. It catches the light. I can feel it pulling at me, drawing me in.

"It's an attention getter, isn't it?" Giavetti says, breaking the spell. I shake my head to clear it, look away.

It's the stone Simon's been going on about. Has to be.

"British stole these babies from the Australian aborigines a hundred years ago, give or take. There are only a couple left in the world. One of them got blown up when a French lieutenant took an artillery shell in World War I. Another one's sitting at the bottom of the ocean. I think some crazy Chinaman ground one of them up and shot it into his dick or something. Then there's this one."

He turns it in the dim light, crazy colors spinning on its surface. "This beauty turned up at a collector's in Beverly Hills. Funny how things turn out, huh? Doesn't look like much, does it?" He kisses the stone, slides it back in his pocket.

"That's it? That's what you hired three guys for? Jesus. You could've gotten a tweaker with a sawed-off cheaper."

"You're telling me. Wouldn't be dealing with this bullshit if I had." He looks at me, waiting for something. When I don't give it to him he sighs. "So, aren't you going to ask? You know you want to."

"Ask what? How that's got a goddamn thing to do with your psychosis?"

He throws up his hands in the air. "You still don't get it. This baby's what makes it all possible. The works, the magilla, the whole shebang. This is the thing that raises the dead, makes you live forever. Hell, I bet it'll shake your dick after you take a leak, if you ask it nice."

"Raise the dead." It sounds insane just coming out of my mouth, but the image of Julio, gray skin and gasping like a fish is worming its way into the foreground. "Really worked great on Julio."

Giavetti's face twists into an ugly frown. "Yeah, the other experiments. They've already fallen apart. But that's what experiments are for, right? I want to use this baby on myself, I got to make sure it works on other people. Got close with your buddy. Damn close. Almost licked that problem with accelerated decomposition and free will."

"Missed a couple ingredients, did you? Not enough nutmeg?"

"Exactly," he says. "It's not like this is a science, you know. More like art. Anyway, I messed up. By the time your buddy tried to take his head off he was already falling apart."

"Bullshit." Julio was fine when I saw him. Already dead, my ass. I remember the blood flowing out of him, the life draining from his eyes. I don't believe it.

"No?" Giavetti says. "Not buying it? Eh, doesn't matter. I'll celebrate anyway."

"Celebrate what?"

"I've done it. Finally. Least, I'm pretty sure I've done it."

His words sink into me. He's done it? The fuck does that mean? Jesus. Let's assume he's not talking smack. That he can pull this off. Crazy and immortal? How do you kill a dead man? How do I stop him from killing me? If this isn't all bullshit, I am seriously fucked. I shove my panic down. Keep him talking. Only way out.

"Yeah? You think that?"

He gives me this look like I'm a lizard in a bell jar. "I don't know," he says. "You tell me."

It takes me a few seconds to register what he's said. And when it does, my world drops out from under me.

I tell myself that I don't feel any different, only I do. My lungs, the missing aches and pains, my blown-out knee. I peel back one of the bandages on my sliced up hands. The cuts are gone.

My body feels like somebody's thrown the off switch but forgot to tell me about it.

Bastard laughs at me again. "Yeah, I'd say I worked out the kinks," he says. He gets up to leave. Stops, slaps his forehead.

"Dammit. I knew I was forgetting something."

He shoots me in the head.

Chapter 5

White hot light. A blast of thunder like sticking my head in a jet engine. I shatter into a thousand pieces, bone and flesh blasting out in a fan behind me.

Everything black. A beat. Maybe two. Then it all snaps back like a rubber band.

My jaw is missing, along with the entire left side of my face. I can feel blood running down my front. I'm blind in one eye. Probably because it's not there anymore.

My right foot spasms, shuddering from the misfired signals it's not getting. I think I can feel a draft on the inside of my skull. Oddly enough, none of this hurts.

Slowly, how slowly I have no idea because my time sense is as fucked as it gets, I can feel things shifting, growing. Brain tissue filling out. Muscle, bone, and skin knitting back together like some crazy aunt's nightmare afghan. Blood spills out of the sealing chasms in my face.

My vision slides back, hearing clears. Teeth coming into a new jaw. Nerves knot themselves back together, firing away happy as chattering fucking magpies. My foot stills.

I have no idea what the hell just happened.

"Well, that was . . . different." Giavetti's looking at me like I just shit out the Vienna Boy's Choir.

It takes me a minute to find my voice. Vocal cords still tying themselves back into their proper knots.

"Gimme the gun," I say, "and I'll show you how it feels from this side."

"Think I'll pass," he says quietly.

"Might want to salt that gun," I say. "Cause when I get out of here I'm gonna feed it to ya."

He says nothing. Just steps backward out of the light from the over-head lamp. The darkness swallows him whole.

I sit there, stunned. My jawbone is lying in my lap along with pieces of pink, rubbery flesh I can't identify. I spit out a couple of old teeth.

Questions. Too goddamn many questions. Can't sort them out for all the noise in my brain. One bubbles to the surface, though. One I don't know how to answer.

Am I dead?

I can't be. I've had my head blown open and sealed back up like a run-flat tire. I'm still moving. I can still think. Cogito ergo fucking sum.

A slow, steady calm settles on me. I'm fine. Have to be. That, or I've completely snapped.

———

It takes me about twenty minutes to screw up my courage. It's not like I haven't done this before. Lots of times.

But it's different when the thumbs you're trying to break are your own.

I yank hard on the handcuffs holding me to the wall, hoping I can find a different way to do it. I'm having trouble focusing. I lose the thread of what I'm doing a couple of times, but eventually I just do it.

I grip my left thumb with the fingers of my right hand, take a deep breath that echoes hollow in my chest, and yank.

It snaps at the joint with a loud crack. Kind of like popping bubble wrap. In the back of my mind I'm nauseated at the sound, but like the bullet to the brain, it doesn't hurt.

With the thumb hanging limp, I worm my hand through the cuff away from the rusty pipe.

Already I feel tendons start to mend, pulling the thumb back into its original position. It takes a few seconds, but when it's done, it may as well have never happened.

I pull myself up from the floor, blood sticking in a thick sheen to my pants where it's pooled beneath me. I snap my other thumb, toss the bracelet to the floor.

First thing is to figure out where the fuck I am. The shower room has seen better days. A long time ago. What's left of the fixtures looks to be from the forties. Same for the tile.

No freeway noise. A virtual impossibility in this town. Up in the Hollywood Hills? No. Place like this would have been bulldozed years ago.

The Santa Monica Mountains? Lots of dead space up there. Place like this might go untouched for a long time. Place like this could be easily forgotten among the canyons and coyotes. One of those places Los Angeles sweeps under the rug, hoping nobody looks at it too closely.

The showers aren't the worst. I stagger through a locker room, metal doors ripped from their hinges. A maze of corridors that zig one way, zag another. Windows boarded over and covered with graffiti. Empty doorways leading to rooms gutted and torched years ago.

Time stretches away from me in a haze. I wander the halls looking for an exit like I'm walking through mud. I'm reaching for something in the back of my mind, but it keeps sliding away like it's on ice.

I need to get out of here. Until I know what the hell's actually happened to me I need to get away from Giavetti. Regroup. Come up with a plan. Get my head together. Maybe literally.

I hang onto that thought. It keeps me going. But somewhere along that dark walk, stumbling over broken furniture and shattered thoughts it comes to me.

I can't leave. Not yet.

My thinking's still muddy, but the brain fog's lifting. Takes a while to rebuild a brain, I suppose. As it does, I find myself thinking more and more about what this all means.

If I've got this right, I can't die. Well, I can't be gotten rid of, at least. I'm like fucking Superman. Go ahead, put a bullet in my brain. Like I goddamn care.

That's kind of cool. But the more my brain comes back online the more it doesn't sound so great.

What happens a hundred years from now? Two hundred? What happens when I'm exactly like this and everything I've ever known is so far away I can barely remember it?

Jesus. Twenty years is a long time. Can I handle two hundred years of not dying? Yeah, probably. I mean, it's not a stretch to think I can just keep plodding along, right? Easier to imagine being here tomorrow than not being here at all.

But something's eating at me. Takes a few minutes to figure out what it is.

Choice. The bastard's taken it away from me. It's not that I necessarily want to go back to what I was. Hell, I just got here. Who knows what this is going to lead to. I might like it, I might not. It's not that I don't want immortality, it's that I want to choose.

The stone's the key to all this. Giavetti couldn't have done this to me without it. Maybe it can reverse it, maybe not. And as long as Giavetti's got it he's got something to hold over me.

I hit a staircase littered with burned-out bed frames and rotting mattresses. I pick my way past the debris, feet crunching on shattered crack pipes, empty beer cans.

The smell hits me halfway up. Rot from the next floor. Meat gone far past bad. A lot of it.

When I get to the top I see why.

Bodies. Half a dozen. Maybe more. Bloated, oozing from splits in the skin. Meat falling off bones. They look weeks old, but I know at least one of them isn't. I can see Julio's dragon tattoos stretched across his back, open sores and maggots swarming around it where the skin has torn. I wonder if his wife is in there, too.

The corpses are piled against the corridor walls, facedown on the floor. I wonder who all those people are and if they're all really dead.

And whether Giavetti even knows what the fuck he's doing.

———

Whispers. A dim light in a room at the end the hallway. Though I'm far off I can see silhouettes. I can pick the voices out as easily as though they were right next to me.

Giavetti. And Simon. Simon, who should be in San Diego.

"We had ourselves a deal," Simon says. "Both of us. I help you get the rock, you do both of us."

"The deal changed," Giavetti says, "the minute you turned on me."

"Goddammit, I didn't do it. I told you that. They saw an opportunity, and they took it."

"Yeah, and who told them about that opportunity? Huh? This was supposed to be kept quiet. All I needed were some men to get the goddamn rock. Men that don't ask questions. I was stupid enough to believe you then. Not this time."

The weight of Simon's betrayal slams into me, and for a moment all I can do is listen, stunned. He knew about all this. Knew where Giavetti was hiding out. Knew what he could do. Would do.

And he threw me to the fucking shark anyway.

I press against the wall, inch my way toward them. Orange shadows flicker around me. Why didn't I see it before? Of course Simon would know. He doesn't make a deal without crawling through every angle. He's had this planned from the start. Let Giavetti take the heat then take the stone for himself.

But it all went to shit, didn't it? Simon hired the guys to steal the stone, but for himself, not for Giavetti. So when Giavetti took them out it left Julio and me to bat cleanup.

"You know it wasn't like that." Simon's voice growing higher, getting frantic. I've never heard him like this. He sounds worse than on the phone when Julio died.

"Right. And that fucking gorilla you sent over the other night? Well, I took care of him, too."

"Jesus. You didn't . . . you didn't have to turn him into a goddamn zombie."

"Oh, I don't know. Between him and your other goon I got things figured out just fine, now."

Silence.

Voice barely a whisper. "What are you talking about?"

"He's talking about me, Simon," I say, stepping into the room.

Giavetti, Beretta in hand. Simon, watching the gun like a mongoose eyeing a cobra.

"Joseph?"

"I guess we know why you wanted that stone so much, huh? That why you're here, Simon? That why you fucked me? Why you fucked Julio? To get your goddamn stone?"

Giavetti lets out a laugh. "Oh, I want to see you talk your way out of this one. On the inside, I'm crying. Really."

"I . . . I was worried. Wanted to make sure—"

I backhand him to the floor, his nose crunching against my knuckles. "You knew about this. The whole fucking time you knew about it. What he was doing. What he could do to us."

"Of course he knew," Giavetti says. "Immortality, son. How do you pass that up?"

"No. I—" Simon's voice trails off as he struggles for air, for something to say. Blood's gushing out of his shattered nose. I grab him by the lapels, lift him above me. He's blubbering, eyes wide. The mongoose just got bit.

I throw him against the wall. Hear something crack. He hits the ground hard, struggles to pull himself up.

"I didn't . . . didn't know," Simon insists. His swollen nose is going purple.

"Don't fucking tell me that," I say. "Tell Julio. Tell his wife." I reach for him, not sure what I'm going to do, knowing it will be final whatever it is.

Giavetti's gunshot makes the decision for me. The bullet punches through Simon's chest, blooming red on his shirt.

Simon scrabbles at the wound, pitches onto his back.

We watch him bleed out. Neither of us makes a move to help him. I'm only sorry I wasn't the one to pull the trigger.

Giavetti and I stare at each other for a long moment, sizing each other up. Hard to tell from the look on his face, but I don't think he's liking his odds much.

"Guess that just leaves us," Giavetti says. He pulls a pack of cigarettes from a pocket, shakes one loose, and tosses the pack to me.

"Go on," he says. "Not like they're going to kill you." He lights up with a Zippo, tosses it to me.

I light up a smoke for myself, take a long drag. Suck down almost half of the thing before I think to take a breath.

Giavetti pulls the opal out of his pocket. Rolls it between knobby fingers. "Got a proposition for you."

"I'm all ears."

"How would you like your life back?"

I stare at him as it sinks in. So he can do it. Or he's just blowing smoke up my ass. I'm leaning toward the smoke theory. But it's a good question. How would I like my life back? Living, I understand. Being dead's going to take some getting used to. But there are some benefits. I work my jaw, feeling tendon and bone, good as new.

But there's that empty feeling, like I've been ripped open and hollowed out. I'm Pinocchio in reverse. The real boy turned into a wooden puppet.

And what if I take him up on his offer? Julio's gone. Simon's gone. Like it or not, nothing's going to be the same.

"What's the catch?" I say. "What do you get out of it?"

"You out of my hair. I bring you back and you go home. Like nothing ever happened."

Yeah, and if you order now you get this handsome Pocket Fisherman. So what if he can do it? What makes me think he will? No. He'd just bring me back and shoot me in the head again. Game over.

"Living forever isn't for lightweights, kid. Something tells me you're not cut out for it. I'm the only one knows how to bring you back. I'm the only one with the answers."

Maybe he's right. Maybe I'm not cut out for it. But I'm not cut out for dying, either.

I glance at Simon's body, dark blood pooling underneath him. He might have screwed me, but he wouldn't have done it if it weren't for Giavetti. "Not sure I trust you much."

He shrugs. "What, and you could trust him? I'm not the one tossed you at me. He was using you as bait, and you know it. So, what'll it be? You want your life back? Then take me up on the deal. You want answers? Only way you're going to get them."

"If you could actually kill me," I say, "you'd have done it already." I take a step toward him. I am so gonna kick his ass.

He raises the gun, like it's going to do any good. "You don't want to do that, kid," he says.

"He's right, Sunday." A familiar voice behind me. "You don't want to do that."

Frank Tanaka steps into the light behind me, gun out and wavering between me and Giavetti. The cavalry's here. Too early or too late, I'm not sure which.

"Well, fuck me," Giavetti says and starts to empty the clip.

Bullets pepper the wall behind us. A round hits me in the chest, another blows out the back of my knee. I go down, my leg buckling under my own weight. I yell at Frank not to fire, but too many years of police work kick in and he takes his shot.

Giavetti's head snaps back with a well placed round. A look, not of rage or fear, just resignation. Like this is just a temporary setback. He wobbles, topples to the floor.

I drag myself to him, try to think of something, anything to help. If he dies, I'm fucked. It's useless.

He's gone.

Chapter 6

"Fuck. Fuck me." Frank runs over, shoves me out of the way. Something wild in his eyes I've never seen before.

He pounds on Giavetti's chest. Starts giving him CPR, like that's going to do any good. The man's missing the entire rear of his skull. Frank's breath just blows out the back.

That's when the stone catches my eye. Under a piece of trash where it skittered when it fell from Giavetti's hand. While Frank's occupied, I snake my hand out and palm it.

There's a surge that runs up my arm like I've hit my funny bone with a sledgehammer. A flare in my vision that swallows everything in a blinding haze of colors. A rush of sound, rising to a deafening pitch. A dazzling light and sound show, patterns shifting, growing, collapsing in on themselves. It goes on forever.

Until it doesn't, leaving behind an abrupt emptiness in my mind. Takes me a moment to come back to myself, realizing that it lasted no time at all. The scene around me hasn't changed.

Frank's muttering to himself, like he's just shot his own dog. Finally he slams his fists on Giavetti's chest and pushes himself away.

"Goddammit." It takes him a second before he seems to notice that I'm still there. And bleeding. "You're hit. I'll—" The slurping sound of my knee regrowing, the gaping hole in my chest collapsing in on itself stops him mid-sentence.

He's sketchy. Can't really blame him, I suppose. But when the bullet in my chest hasn't even finished popping out, he loses his shit and puts another one right back in.

"Jesus, man. Do you mind?" My ears are ringing. He's taken out my left lung, and my voice is a wheezy gasp. I'm really going to have to burn these clothes.

I pull myself up from the floor, the new knee still unsteady. At that range the hole's big enough to shove a grapefruit through. I don't want to know what the back looks like. "Just put the fucking gun down. I've been shot enough today, thank you."

Frank lowers the pistol. His eyes glued to the already closing wound.

I put my hand out. He stares at it. "Get up." Slowly, he takes it. I haul him to his feet.

"Nice shot," I say.

"Thanks."

"I don't think he's dead." If Simon gutting him in the fifties didn't do it, I doubt this will either.

"Yeah, I know."

"He's— What do you mean, you know?"

Frank opens his mouth to say something but the radio on his belt squawks, announcing that backup's on the way. ETA's ten minutes. The hard resolve I'm used to comes back into his eyes.

"You. Out of here. Hang a right down the hall. I'll cover for you. Your car's up the hill. Key's in the ignition." He shoves me toward the door.

"The hell?" Not complaining, but I don't know what's going on.

"I don't need you in an interrogation room. We'll talk later."

Like that's going to happen. Must be reading my mind because he grabs my shoulder, leans in.

"Don't skip out on me," he says.

"Give me a reason."

"Because you want to know what I know."

Dammit.

———————

I head home to my place near La Brea and Fountain. Bought it with cash about ten years ago. Little two bedroom Spanish cottage with bars on the windows. Not a bad place. Quiet neighborhood, all things considered. The only gunfire on my street happens during the holidays when idiots citywide decide that shooting in the air is the best way to celebrate Jesus being born.

I need to clean up, sure, but first I have to stash this goddamn stone. Pockets are a bad place for anything. Shit falls out, you forget it's there. First thing I do is hide the stone in a safe in the back of my closet. Also not the best place to stash something. It's not a great safe, hinges on the outside. A good couple of hours with a crowbar and the door will probably pop off. But until I can think of a better place, it's what I've got.

I stash my clothes in a trash bag to burn later. Scrub the blood and gore off my body until the shower runs cold, though I barely notice the temperature. Spend a good hour afterward staring at the wall wondering what to do with all this jittery energy I've got. It's been at least twenty-four hours since I slept last, but I'm not tired. Makes a weird sort of sense. I'm dead, right? Don't need to breathe, don't need to sleep?

Sitting around is not something I'm good at. I pull on some gym clothes, throw together a bag, and head out the door. I need to burn off some of this energy.

Friend of mine, Carl Reed, runs a gym out of a strip mall in Hollywood between a roach-infested Ukrainian restaurant and a Starbucks. Old world, new world, fighting in between.

Carl inherited the place from his old man, Chuck "The Hammer" Reed, a couple years back. Chuck fought heavyweight in the early seventies while Carl and I were going to high school together. Spent years brawling his way to the title until a detached retina brought all that to a halt. So he opened the gym and taught.

I give Carl a nod as I come in. I've been training here since his dad opened the place. In some ways I spent more time with his father than Carl did. Carl went off to college. Didn't want to end up like his old man so he did the exact opposite. Got a degree in English and went on to be a reporter. Now he works at the *Times*. He has a guy run the gym for him, but keeps an office in the back. Doesn't want to sell the place. Closest thing to a legacy he's ever going to get.

Just a handful of guys in the gym going through their routines. I feel the need to beat the crap out of something. Carl comes over while I'm taping my hands, grabs the roll, and finishes it up.

"You always sucked putting this shit on," he says, his deep bass rumble sounding just like his old man's.

I give him a grin. "This stuff's for pussies anyway," I joke.

"Yeah," he says. "Real men like busted hands." He finishes the job, tightens the Velcro on my gloves.

"How's the newspaper business?"

"Internet's kicking its ass," he says. "Not to mention the latest rich, white asshole who bought it. How's the thug business?"

Now that's a loaded question. I know what he's really asking: "Is there anything you can give me?" Every once in a while I bounce some tidbit over to him that finds its way into the paper. I'm an official Anonymous Source. Carl's known what I do for a long time. Mostly. I don't talk about the killing. Just roughing people up. He doesn't pry, just takes what I give him.

I wish I could tell him, but I don't know where to start.

"Pretty quiet lately," I say.

Carl's got a military grade bullshit detector, and I know I just set it off. He cocks an eyebrow but doesn't say anything. "If it heats up, let me know," he says. "Could use some fodder for the fish wrapper." He leaves to go check on some kid who's having trouble with a speed bag.

I head over to one of the heavy bags in the corner, let myself get lost in the sound of gloves on leather drowning out the sounds of boxing all around me. Guys in the ring, jumping rope, hitting the speed bag. Time goes by. How much I can't say. I'm just hitting the bag.

Carl pokes his George Foreman face around the bag. "Dude, what are you on?" he asks.

"What?" I hammer at the bag again, try to get back into my groove. The smack of leather on leather.

"I'm talkin' about the Popeye number you got going here. You've been hogging this bag over an hour. You haven't stopped moving. You on something stronger than spinach?"

I stop, step back. An hour? I glance over my shoulder at the clock, catch the weirded-out stares of the other guys. I hadn't noticed the time.

"Fuck, man. I had no idea."

"Yeah. You know, you're not even breathing hard." I take a breath, hope he doesn't catch on that I wasn't breathing at all. He swipes a finger across my forehead, shows it to me. "And you aren't sweating, either. Fact, you're as cold as ice. What's going on?"

"Dude, you're always worried about me. Just had a rough night's all."

Another ping on the bullshit detector. "Yeah, well, shake it up a little. Hit the speed bag, do some weights. This shit's freaking out the paying customers."

I nod. He's right. I'm going to have to watch myself. Too much of this, and I'm going to get questions I can't answer.

I do a circuit. My usual workout. Only there's no strain. The weights are heavy, sure, but the only thing giving me a problem is the integrity of my bones and muscles. Not fatigue, not pain. When I think nobody's looking I slide on some more weights and bench 500. My top's 350.

The whole time I'm thinking about fitting in. I'm different now. No two ways about it. I can't just go on like nothing's happened, but I can't let anyone know. Jesus, what would people do if they found out?

But how *do* I fit in? It feels like trying to walk drunk. All those little balance moves your body just does and you never think about. And then you get hammered and have to think about them. Can I make my heart beat? I can breathe, but my lungs are just windbags.

The big things are easy to hide, but people pick up on the little things. How many of those little details am I missing? I throw in some grunts as I hit the bags, but I'm not feeling it, and if nobody notices that I'd be surprised.

I catch a view of myself in the mirror. I look all right, if a little haggard. But then I'm getting old. I always look haggard. Not sweating, not getting tired. What else am I missing? My head starts to spin with all the things I'm forgetting. After a while I just stop. No point in getting more worked up. Not like I can do anything about it.

I stow my gear in my bag, pretend to wipe sweat off my face with a towel, and head to the door. Carl's shadow looms behind me.

"Hang on, he says. "You and me have to talk." He takes me back to his office, closes the door. Flicks on an old RCA sharing space with a bamboo plant on top of his filing cabinet. Staticky picture, a local channel, comes up with some talking head going off about the Middle East. Dude really needs to get cable in here.

"You're not gonna show me your homemade porn movies again, are ya? I can only handle seeing your johnson so many times."

"Only way you're seeing my meat's when I'm stone cold dead, and you know it. You want a sausage fest go down a couple blocks on a Saturday night. Now shut up and wait for it. Big news. Just saw it. Bound to come around again."

We watch. The usual horseshit. Oil, fighting, genocide. Gangbangers shooting up kids in parks, home invasions getting grannies killed. It's depressing shit. Why I stopped watching TV years ago. A couple commercials go by. Makes me wonder why Giavetti was so fired up about living forever. It's not like the world gets any better.

"Here we go," Carl says, turns up the volume.

LAPD cars, yellow tape. A canyon in the Santa Monica Mountains. And a picture of Simon.

"Fuck." Of course it would make the news.

"You knew about this?" Carl asks.

"What? Fuck no. When did it happen?"

Carl is silent a moment longer than he should be, and I know I've been made. "Cops found them this morning. Whole slew of bodies. Like some Jonestown shit or something." Interesting angle Frank came up with. Crazy cultists gone bugfuck. Something for the press to chew on.

"Jesus."

"Looks like you're out of a job."

"Looks like."

"You don't seem too broken up."

"What? Hell, man, it's kind of a shock. Gimme some time to sort it out."

"Horseshit," he says.

"Oh, come on," I say. "You think I'd be here if I knew this had gone down?"

"As a matter of fact, yes," he says. "I know you do more than just rough up people who don't pay. I'm not stupid, Joe. I know how to put facts together. I'm a fucking reporter. It's my job. I think you'd just go about your day like you always do. Now, what the hell happened?"

"Don't ask me this, man," I say. "I don't need more shit in the paper than what's already in there."

His face twists in anger. "Jesus. I'm your friend, you asshole."

"And what, nothing's gonna end up plastered on the front page? I'm not stupid, either."

He stands, more pissed off than I've seen him in years. "Fuck you," he says. "This is too big to just go on your fucking day with. You didn't hear the first part. They found more than twenty bodies in there."

"Don't," I say.

He gets into my face. "Why not? You gonna take me out? Is that what you're all freaked out about? You kill those people? I got a fucking mass murderer in my gym today?"

I don't even think about it, I just throw a punch and pop him in the jaw. I don't think I put a lot of force into it but it knocks him back into the door, a spiderweb crack appearing in the wired glass where his head hits.

Carl steadies himself, shakes it off. Blood is running down his chin, his split lip already fattening. He makes to come at me, but stops himself.

"Get out," he says.

"Carl, I—"

"You don't want to tell me," he says, cutting me off, "that's your business. I'll find out on my own."

"Man, you do not want to—"

"I said get out," he screams. He throws the door open and steps aside to let me pass. The gym is silent, everyone watching me as I walk out.

If they didn't notice me before they sure as hell do now.

———

I spend the rest of the day driving around town. Not wanting to go home and look at that goddamn stone again. It's like it wants me to pull it out and stare at it.

Everything looks different. Colors are a little sharper, sounds a little more clear. And the smells. Jesus. I can smell everything. I didn't notice it until after I left the gym, but I'm starting to smell people like they're bags of meat.

And I'm getting paranoid. Keep seeing this black Escalade popping in and out of traffic behind me. This is L.A., everybody's got a fucking black Escalade. After awhile I settle down, stop seeing it.

My phone rings. It's Carl. I turn off the ringer. I'm going to have to talk to him soon, though. Tell him something if only for damage control. With Frank covering for me I should be good with the cops for the moment, but I'm going to have to do something to keep Carl from digging too much into this thing.

Wish I hadn't lost it back there. Now it's just going to be that much more difficult to keep a lid on things.

I finally drive to the coast, up along Pacific Coast Highway, past Malibu, toward the crime scene. News vans are crowded along the side of the road a good mile from the site. I hang farther back. Far enough away to be another looky-loo, close enough to maybe actually see something. I strain to see past the crush of reporters. I can see the police, the ambulances. They've already hauled the bodies away, but it's going to be awhile before they're done here. Coroner's going to be busy tonight.

I watch them until the sun goes down and everybody but the hardcore has gone home. I don't take a breath for four hours.

I check my phone. It tells me I've got three messages. Two from Carl sounding almost apologetic but still pissed off. And one from Frank.

It's a simple message. A place and time. Hard edge in his voice that I'm used to. Says he wants answers.

I'd like a few myself.

Chapter 7

I meet Frank at Mel's in Sherman Oaks later that night. White ceramic mugs of coffee between us, smell of fry grease in the air. A large manila envelope sitting conspicuously on the table.

The place is overlit with hanging fluorescents, Fifties music piped in over a crackling sound system. Lots of people here. Lots of witnesses. Takes me a few minutes to realize that he's more afraid of me than I am of him.

I've been avoiding the question, but I can't anymore. "You said you knew Giavetti wasn't dead. He get up and start walking around?"

"If he does we'll know about it. I've got him in the morgue."

"Well, that's something."

The silence stretches in front of us. "Everything cool?" Frank finally asks.

"I'm not gonna eat your brain, if that's what you're asking." I've got a burger in front of me, but after a few tentative bites, I'm just not interested. Hungry, though, which I didn't expect.

"Good to know." He hasn't touched his food.

"So, is this where the thrilling detective pulls out his whodunit card and fills me in on everything?"

"Was hoping you'd brought yours," he says.

I pat my pockets. "Must be in that other jacket. You know, the one with the big fuckin' hole in it."

"What were you doing there?"

"You asking as a cop?"

He shakes his head. "No badge. Must be in my other jacket."

I have to be careful. Weigh every word. What to tell him, what not to. I've never cracked for him before, I'm not about to start now. He's staring at me, waiting. Not his cop stare. Something more earnest, more pained.

Fuck it. Everything's different, now.

"Dying," I say finally. "Coming back to life. Fuck, I don't know." I tell him about the phone call to Mariel, finding Julio at his home, Giavetti, the strangulation. Coming to in the shower room. He nods to himself like I'm filling in pieces of a puzzle I didn't know I had.

"And you just woke up? Just like that?"

"Pretty much. Then he shot me in the head."

"That must have sucked."

"Not as bad as you'd think. His rant was worse." Now it's my turn. "What about you? How'd you find me?"

"Luck mostly," he says. "I've been keeping tabs on him since I knew he was in town. Tailed him there the other day. Didn't get a chance to get inside, though. Figured that was the best place to start." He shudders. "No offense, but I wish I'd never gone in there."

"Saw the bodies, did ya?"

"Fuck. Julio was in that pile, wasn't he?"

I nod. "Think so. Thought I saw his tattoos. What's the count?"

"Twenty-five last time I checked. They're still digging through it all."

"Got a question for ya," he says and reaches into the manila envelope, rummages around, and comes out with a photo of the stone. The picture doesn't do it justice. "When you were in there, you see this?"

I shake my head. "Should I have?"

"Don't know. It was stolen a while back from a guy in Bel Air. Word is that Giavetti hired some muscle through Simon to snag it."

"So that's what all the noise is about," I say, hoping I'm not laying it on too thick. I tell him about the bad blood between Giavetti and Simon over the guys who've gone missing. I leave out the bits about Simon knowing Giavetti from way back when. "I didn't know Giavetti'd hired guys to get a stone, though."

"You never asked?"

"I look like the kind of guy who does that?"

He snorts. "Guess not. You know, it's funny. I've been trying to nail your ass to the wall for years now. Now that I've got something I could lay on you, it turns out I can't do anything with it. You'd probably just yawn through the gas chamber now, wouldn't you?"

I ignore him and ask, "So what's so special about this stone?"

"Fuck if I know. Was hoping you did." He gives me a hard cop stare. "You're not lying to me, are you?"

"Cross my heart, hope to die."

"Bullshit."

"I love you, too."

"Fine." He's mulling something over, chewing on his lip. He empties the manila envelope onto the table. Papers, photos. He sifts through them, pulls one out.

"This is my kid brother, Leonard," he says. It's easy to see the resemblance. Younger, thinner. Looks like a happy guy, doesn't have Frank's Eeyore face.

"He got the looks."

"Yeah, tell me about it. Brains, too. Valedictorian. Graduate degree. FBI. He'd been trying to put together a case on a group operating out of Chicago. All he could get were small operators. Bagmen, shit like that. But Giavetti's name kept popping up."

"Popular guy."

"You'd think, only nobody's actually seen him. Like he's Bigfoot or the Jersey Devil. Folks can't, or won't, give a description. Like they've, I dunno, forgotten what he looks like, where he hangs out. So Lenny digs. Takes him a while but he finally gets hold of a picture."

He pulls a copy of an old sepia photo. Older guy, derby on his head. Give him a different haircut and we've got the zombie master himself.

"You're kidding me," I say.

"Big family, the Giavettis. In Italy. In the states there's maybe a dozen of them left. Lenny scoured every state and federal record he could get his hands on. Every one of them a bust."

The waitress comes by, coffee pot in hand. Cute redhead in a bobby sox outfit, hair pulled up behind a little paper hat. Frank puts his hands over the uncovered photos like they're state secrets.

"More coffee?" Her Southern accent's a little too thick for someone who's been here long. Girl next door look. Actress, most likely. Probably bit parts, if she can get them. Maybe some repertory. If she's not careful, this place will eat her up.

"I'm good, thanks," Frank says.

I put my cup out. I don't know why. I'm not interested in the coffee at all. Barely touched it. But there's enough room to top it off. She bends over to pour. She smells good.

"Hi," I say. I catch her eyes. Green like jade. "Nice eyes."

She graces me with a dazzling smile. "Thanks." I watch her as she walks off, a little extra sway in her hips just for me.

"The fuck are you doing?"

"What? I just told her I liked her eyes."

"You're hitting on the waitress."

I remember the exchange between him and the woman officer back at the station. "You're fucking another cop," I say. He pauses at this. Blinks.

"I'm not dead."

Yeah, okay. He has me there. And then there's also the fact that I don't normally go after waitresses. Strippers, barflies, sure. One time even a roller derby queen. God, she was fun. But some fresh-faced twenty-year-old? That's not like me.

My stomach rumbles loud enough for Frank to hear.

"You hungry?"

I ignore the question. "So the picture," I say, trying to get the conversation back on track.

"Yeah. So he talks to everybody he possibly can. Background checks. Even taps their phones. Nothing. So he starts from today and works his way back."

"And he finds this? What the hell was he gonna do with it?"

"They've got a computer at Quantico that matches faces in photos. Still experimental. Guess part of it's hooked to the Smithsonian or something. Anyway, he runs it through and gets a whole slew of hits. Only they're not what he's expecting."

He pulls out a half dozen photos from different eras. Spreads them out in front of me.

"Jesus." Giavetti stares at me out of every one of them.

Frank taps each one in turn. "Abilene, 1875. Chicago, 1902. Tulsa, 1914. Miami, 1928. Sacramento, 1937. New York, 1942." Hair's a little different. Going backward he's a little younger, but not by much. Ten years, fifteen? Sometimes he's in a group, sometimes alone. But it's the same guy every time.

"There's more, but I think you get the idea. Every decade there's a guy looks just like him. Little bit younger. Usually goes with a different name, but Lenny was able to correlate some birth and death dates and had a pretty good idea it was all the same guy."

"He doesn't look much different than he did when you shot him."

"Yeah. I've got some ideas on that, but I'm not sure. So, anyway, when the system gets back online Lenny runs it again and gets this."

Hands me a printout of an Illinois driver's license. Old man Giavetti staring at me over the name Samuel Glen Vetty. Boy's got no imagination.

"So how come it's you out here tracking down Giavetti and not your brother?"

"He's dead. Died a few years ago."

"Bummer."

Frank's hand clenches into a fist. If he's looking for sympathy, he knows I'm the wrong guy to go to.

"The feds had already dropped the case and he was on to bigger and better things, but he couldn't get this out of his head. I found all this in his apartment after he died."

"Wait a minute. Your kid brother goes all Kolchak the Night Stalker, and now you're picking up the cause? What gives?" It takes me a second to answer my own question. "Giavetti killed him."

"Yeah. He turned up dead in a warehouse run by some guys with connections to Giavetti."

It's sketchy at best. No way he'd be able to prove a damn thing in court, and really, how would you even get it to that point? No, he's not interested in trying to bring him in. He's stepped outside the bounds of his badge. It's weird to see him on my side of the fence.

"You want to kill him. You sure he's not already dead? You said his body's in the morgue."

"Please," Frank says. "The man's been around long enough, I don't think a bullet to the head's going to slow him down too much."

I have a sudden thought. "Well, fuck, then why'd you send him to the morgue?"

"The fuck was I supposed to do? Shove him into my trunk with sheriffs all over the place? Yeah, that'd really work out well. 'Don't mind me. guys, just taking this guy in for questioning.' Fuck you, I'm not stupid. Morgue's the best place for him. If he's not really dead he's gonna be awful surprised when they crack him open tomorrow and scoop his guts out. And if he gets up in the middle of the night somebody'll see him."

He's right. I don't like it, but I can't see what else he could have done. Cops were coming up the canyons as I was heading out. Frank wouldn't have had much time to move the body.

I look at the pictures. Giavetti's old in all of them. "If these are right he's been around for, what, a hundred-fifty years?"

Frank shakes his head. "Worse. Lenny thought he's aging about a year for every ten or so."

I do some quick math in my head. I don't like the number I'm coming up with. "That's not possible," I say, knowing how stupid that sounds coming from me.

Frank looks through the envelope, pulls one last picture out, and lays it face up on the table like a cardsharp at a high stakes poker game.

It's Giavetti again. Only he's younger. A lot younger. And he's looking out at me from the middle of a Renaissance painting.

Chapter 8

I pull out onto Ventura Boulevard, the neon signs of furniture stores and Italian restaurants lighting up the night in reds and blues.

Frank's got no real answers, only more questions. The only way I'll be getting any is through Giavetti. His body's cooling in the morgue, but God only knows if he's coming back or not. I'm still on the fence about this whole living forever thing. But if Frank's right then Giavetti's probably going to be up and walking around soon. Gives me hope of getting some answers. And if I have to make Giavetti hurt to get them, so much the better.

I'm antsy, restless. Like I was when I headed over to Carl's gym, but there's something else. Some new edge to it I can't put my finger on. I drive over the hill into Hollywood looking for something. I've gone through half a pack, and I'm not even at Mulholland. My stomach growls at me, but every kind of food I can think of makes me queasy.

I pass bars on Sunset, long lines of men and women all looking to get laid snaking outside along the sidewalks. Though I'm not in the mood for a drink, every time I pass one it grabs my attention like somebody's set off a flare. The street corners are brimming with whores. The cops make a sweep every now and again, but they'll never clear them out.

I pass a strip bar off a corner of Hollywood Boulevard. The place has really gone downhill, if it was ever up one. Peeling paint, half the flashing bulbs in its sign out or blinking out of sequence. There are a handful of cars in the lot, a couple girls out front smoking. A brunette in a miniskirt and fishnets catches my eye. Waitress or a dancer. But a strip bar's not what I'm looking for, either.

Or maybe it is. A few blocks later I make a U-turn and head back.

The brunette's still out front. She's sharp enough to notice the same car passing by. Really gets her attention when I double back from the other direction.

I don't see any cops, though if she is one she'll have a wire to call a team of guys in a van around the block. I circle the area looking for anything that catches my eye. Nothing.

I pull into the lot, leave the engine running. Find myself drumming the steering wheel with my fingers. What the hell am I doing here? My thoughts are interrupted by a tap on the driver's side window. It's the brunette. I didn't even notice her come up.

She's got a face, heroin thin, hair teased up like she's auditioning for a Whitesnake video. She was pretty once. A long time ago. I roll down the window, and her scent hits me like a hammer. Like chocolate chip cookies, sex, and steak all rolled into one. Jesus.

"Hey, sugar," she says.

"Hey." I can barely talk. I just want to breathe in her scent. Awkward silence when I don't say anything else.

"You, uh, you lookin' for a party?" she says. I pull myself back.

"Yeah," I say without thinking. "You free?"

She laughs. "No, but I am a bargain. Got a nice quiet spot out in the back if you're looking for something quick." She snakes her tongue around too red lipstick, over crooked teeth. "These lips'll take you to a whole other world."

"Not out here," I say. "You got a place nearby?"

"That'll cost you," she says.

I pull a couple hundreds from my wallet and show her. "How's that?" She's almost drooling. So am I.

"That'll work." She plucks the bills from my fingers and gets into the car.

———

"What are you into, sugar?" she asks.

"This and that," I say. Might be into a lot of things but this isn't one of them. I don't know why I'm doing this, but I can't seem to stop myself.

She steers me to a motel, and I pull into a darkened alley out of sight of the rooms.

"I get a lot of those," she says and gets out of the car. I follow her to a room near the back, the walkway barely lit by broken lights. She's got long legs and a slight limp. Like a wounded gazelle.

"Pretty quiet here," I say. My voice sounds like gravel in my ears.

"Won't nobody bother us, sugar," she says. "You can make all the noise you want." She opens the door, flicks on a light. It's a small room. Bed, bathroom, nasty green carpet. Empty bottle of Stoli lying on the small table in the corner, a box of Trojans on the nightstand.

"So, how about we—" she stops when she gets a good look at me in the light. "Hey now," she says. "You on something? It's cool if ya are, but I don't want no crazy shit here, understand me?"

I don't know what the hell she's talking about until I catch sight of myself in the mirror across from the bed. I look like hell. My face is gaunt, color a shade of pale one notch above fish-belly white. The skin around my eyes and lips has sunk in.

"I'm fine," I say. "I just need a minute." I go into the bathroom and shut the door.

I stare at myself in the bathroom for god knows how long and watch my face fall in on itself. It's like one of those time lapse films they show you in high school of what happens when mushrooms grow.

My skin turns gray green, sags around the eyes, recedes from my fingernails. Blisters form on my face. Yellow pus beads on my skin. My cheek splits, oozing thick liquid.

Three weeks of dead man in two minutes flat.

My stomach twists into a knot. I double over. Christ, I could eat the fucking walls.

Or something else.

I have to get out of here. I have to get away from the whore in the other room or, hell, I don't know what I'll do.

The only openings in the room are the door or a tiny air vent over the toilet. No joy there. Maybe I can bum rush her, knock her out of the way. Get out before it gets much worse.

"You okay, sugar?" she calls through the door.

"Don't come in," I say. But it's a wheezy rattle. My tongue is thick and slimy. One of my molars falls out.

She cracks the door open. I grab the handle, ready to run. She gets a good look at me and screams.

I flash back on Julio going after the bartender, how he was trying to rip through the guy's sternum.

I want to run but I grab her instead. My fingers, the skin sloughing off to show bone underneath, dig into the flesh of her shoulders.

She's not some down on her luck whore anymore. Some girl who does too much heroin and has to feed a bad habit.

I look at her, and all I see is meat.

———

There's something warm and sticky on the bathroom floor, matted in my hair, soaked into my clothes. I feel like I've been shit through a rhino.

The room's dark, and I pretend for a second that I'm just having a bad dream. I peel myself from the floor, not sure how much time has passed. A minute? An hour? I don't hear breathing. Did she get away? Did I let her go?

My hand searches for the light switch and, when I find it, I get my answer. She's propped up in the bathtub, empty eyes staring straight ahead, a hole in her chest you could cram a bowling ball into. Her sternum juts from cracked ribs, one partially chewed breast hangs by a scrap. Intestines drape in tattered loops from the bottom of the hole.

Her heart's gone.

The bathroom is dripping with gore. Blood streaks the walls, pools on the floor. I can't figure out where all the meat that's been scooped out of her chest has gone, and I can only come up with one explanation.

Not only am I dead, I'm a cannibal. One more reason to kick the shit out of Giavetti.

I wipe enough of the blood from my face to see myself clearly. Not only have I stopped rotting, but it's like it never happened. Skin's the right color, teeth aren't feeling loose in their sockets anymore. This is Giavetti's idea of immortality?

"Holy fuck," I whisper and nearly jump out of my skin when the whore's head moves to track my voice.

So this is what a horror movie looks like from the inside.

———

A maid's cart is a killer's best friend. Bleach, mops, extra towels. If you can't clean a room with it you can light the damn thing on fire. I find one down the hall. It takes a couple of hours, but by the time I'm done with the bathroom it's cleaner than before the gorefest started.

I find some men's clothes in the closet. The pants hike up about three inches above my ankles, but they fit well enough around my waist. A trenchcoat covers me up but the shoes are a lost cause. Toss my own blood-soaked mess into a trash bag and hope to hell I can get everything finished before whoever's clothes I'm wearing comes home.

Go over the checklist in my head: bathroom's cleaned, clothes are changed, I showered to get most of the blood and mess off of me. Only thing left is to figure out what to do with the whore's body.

On the one hand, moving her should be a snap. Most of her blood is down the drain, and I've got the hole packed with half a dozen towels. Could just walk her out to my car.

On the other hand, what do I do with her then? Put a bullet in her head like the movies or is she enough like me that that'll just heal? The hole in her gut hasn't, so maybe not. But what the fuck do I know about this stuff?

I look her over, trying to understand what's happened to her, what I've done to her. The spark in her eyes is gone. She's got the same cold fish look I got from Julio before he choked the life out of me.

God help her if she's still in there.

I've kept a pretty good hold on the whole situation so far, treating it like any other job, if a lot more bloody than most. But that thought does it, and the whole fucking thing finally hits me. I start shaking, dry heave over the toilet.

A few minutes later I pull myself together. Everybody gets the shakes sometimes. But I need to be done with it now. It's not helping.

A jacket from the closet goes over her shoulders. I'll get her in the car and see where we go from there. Take it one step at a time.

Stand her up, walk her over to the door. The sound of keys jangling in the lock stops me. I draw my gun just as the door opens to a wiry Asian guy in a Dodgers cap and a gray hoodie. He barely glances at me, but his eyes lock on her.

He jabs a finger at her, yelling in a shriek that smacks of English-as-a-second-language, "Where the fuck have you been? This asshole better fucking be the last in a long line of blow jobs tonight. You were supposed to be on your goddamn corner over an—"

I grab the back of his head and shove his face into the butt of my pistol, breaking his nose with a loud pop. Throw him onto the bed, kick the door closed behind him. It's a slight change in plan, but not a problem. Plenty of room in my trunk for him, too.

I turn, ready to take care of him just as the whore does it for me.

She leaps on him, growling. Clamps her jaws tight around his neck. He doesn't have a chance to scream before she tears his throat out. Blood spurts as she hits the carotid. He thrashes, beats at her head, kicks the air. Nothing helps.

"Goddamn it, cut it out," I say. She's making a mess of the room. I pull on her, but it's like trying to dislodge a tick. I can't get her off him. I pistol whip her hard enough to crack bone. Grab the bedside lamp, smash it down onto her head. Does fuck all to her.

Hope she was right about how much noise somebody could make around here. Blow a hole into her skull with my Glock.

A chunk of brain the size of my fist flies across the room. Her left arm twitches. She stops a moment. Just when I think it's over, goes back to chewing his head off.

I shove the barrel through the hole in her skull and pop off another round. It blows through the front of the guy's face, spraying their brains across the bed.

She convulses and flops down hard onto the body of her dead pimp.

Jesus fuck. Even Julio wasn't this hard to slow down.

The room's a mess. I can't risk the time to clean it up. I start to wrap them up in the bedsheets, thinking I can haul them out over my shoulder and get out fast. Then the pimp tries to sit up.

"Oh, for fuck's sake." No way in hell he could be alive. His head's barely hanging on. I grab the top of his skull and yank, snapping his neck. He shakes like an epileptic, falls back down onto the bed.

I finish wrapping them up in the sheets. This part of town cops'll look it over, chalk it up to one more L.A. tragedy.

———

Getting them out is easier than I expected. A window leads to the alley. My car's got a big trunk, and I've got a plastic drop cloth. Never know when you're going to need one of those.

I hit the freeway. There's a gravel quarry off the 605 in Monrovia. Guy who runs it, Pedro, knows me from work I've done for Simon. Owes me a couple favors for not squawking about his selling bodies for organs to a Chinese buyer in Gardena.

I give him a call. He's just woken up, but when I tell him I've got a delivery he tells me he'll be there to let me in.

Pedro stares at my outfit when I get out of the car, but he doesn't say anything about it. Helps me haul the wrapped up bodies and trashbags out of my trunk. He'll use a forklift to run them over to the loading bin of a rock crusher and let it pulverize them.

The two corpses fall heavily onto a wooden pallet and the sheets open up, the whore rolling out onto the gravel. The wad of towels stuffed into her chest falls out. Pedro gives a little yell and crosses himself.

"The fuck happened to her?" he asks.

"Shit," I say. "Shit happened." I roll her back onto the palette, pull the sheets back over her. "Come on, gimme a hand here."

He steps back. "I'm not fucking touching her. What does that to a person? That's not normal. Nothing normal does that to a person."

I grab him, shove my Glock into his face. "Shut up," I say. "Shut your goddamn mouth and maybe you won't go in there with her. Got me?"

He eyes the gun, nods.

I throw the rest of the cash I have at his feet, about five hundred dollars. "Take the money. Do your job. Forget about this."

"Looks like a monster did this," he says.

"Yeah," I say and leave.

Chapter 9

I lit a guy on fire once.

He thrashed around a good twenty minutes before he died. Screaming the whole time until the smoke from his own body choked the air out of him. Then he just gurgled as his skin turned black and crackled like old paper.

I used a nailgun to pin his wrists to a chunk of new drywall at a construction site outside of Bakersfield so he wouldn't roll around. Then I lit him on fire, and I watched him burn.

Until tonight that was at the top of my Worst Things I've Ever Done list.

I scrub myself raw. Brush my teeth until my gums shred. Go through two bottles of Listerine. I'm not sure it'll ever be enough.

It's almost midnight. I've been dead almost twenty-four hours. I'm not sure how I feel about that.

I'm still not tired. Guess that's not really a surprise. Been going all day like I'm buzzing on a tank of coffee. Not feeling any signs of slowing down. So much for resting in peace.

My cell rings while I'm getting dressed. Danny calling from Simon's club. Guess it's his now.

"Yeah," I say.

"You've heard, right?" Danny says, a thudding techno bass line in the background. "Tell me you've heard."

"I heard," I say. "This afternoon. It was on the news."

"Shit's moving fast, man. I got calls in from the Armenians, the Israelis, some guy I think is Yakuza. I can barely understand him. You gotta come in, man. We need to have a heart-to-heart."

"The fuck are you talking about?"

"The future. The future that's happening right the fuck now. Simon's gone, man. What, you want to work for the fucking Armenians? 'Cause that's what's gonna happen if we don't have a powwow and get our shit together."

"Christ, Danny, the corpse isn't even cold, yet."

"That's my point," he says. "The buzzards are out in force, and I need to establish things now."

"What do you want from me? It's over, Danny. All things considered I'd just as well hang it up. I got other shit going on."

"Look," he says. "I get it. The old man was your friend, we're all buddy-buddy, but all I'm asking is that you come in, and let's have a conversation. Face-to-face. Is that too much to ask?"

I haven't thought about my job prospects. Had more pressing things on my mind. "Fine," I say. "I'll swing by."

"Thanks, man. I appreciate it." I can hear the relief in his voice.

"Sure. That it?"

"Yeah," he says. "No. Wait. Some guy came in looking for you. Something about a stone. Said it was important. I told him to fuck off but he said he'd be by later. This something I should be worried about?"

I think about that for a minute. Somebody's looking for Giavetti's stone? I'm not sure if this is good or bad.

"Yo, earth to Sunday. You there?" he asks.

"It's cool." I say. "Side gig. Didn't know I'd get a caller at the club is all. He say who he was?"

"No," Danny says. "Didn't leave a name. So, this isn't some leftover job for Simon? Because if it is . . . ."

"No. Personal. He say when he was coming by?"

"Just later tonight."

"All right. I'll be out there before you guys shut down."

"Thanks man. I owe you." He hangs up.

I figured somebody else had to know about the stone. Some shit you just can't keep secret. And if they know about the stone, maybe they know how to use it.

I reload the Glock, slide it into its shoulder rig. I'm pretty sure I can convince them to tell me.

———

I make it up to Hollywood Boulevard in a few minutes. It's a weird place at night. Homeless guy pissing on Marilyn Monroe's star, Scientologists waving their pamphlets around and screaming at people about their engrams. Simon's club is off a side street between Highland and Vine.

There's a line outside the door that stretches twenty feet down the block. From the crowd I'd say it's bondage night. The name changes based on the theme. Tonight it's Bête Noir.

The crowd is mostly tourists looking for a thrill and a few in the scene. The club is legit, but that's not where it makes its money.

Lots of leather. Corsets, thigh-highs, the latest in latex evening wear. A floor show to keep things interesting. Pretty boys and girls tied to crosses, bent over racks.

As long as there aren't any nipples or bush, and nobody's actually fucking on stage, the vice squad leaves them pretty much alone. It helps that half the officers who come in are on the take.

I cut to the front of the line, flag down Bruno, one of the bouncers. Built like a Russian wrestler with a nose flatter than a tire on a bed of nails. I've worked with him when we needed a little more firepower than Julio and I could pack. Good in a fight, but I've never been entirely clear on who paid him—Simon or Danny.

Bruno nods, pulls back the black velvet rope for me. A group of girls, push-up bras and overdone makeup screaming jailbait, are all bitched off until Bruno picks a couple to come on in. A woman in purple leather and thigh-high boots escorts them to the back like they're VIPs.

Smart money says they'll be somebody's private floor show before morning.

The club is a converted warehouse. Three main rooms, each with its own bar. Cement floors, exposed ducts. Wired glass in the louvered windows, all painted over black.

I see the floor show the minute I walk through the curtains in the foyer. Muted spotlights make the stage glow in the center of the main room. A redhead with a back tat of wings across her shoulders and black tape over her tiny breasts lies blindfolded over a padded sawhorse, ass in the air.

The dom's a guy in a tux and a carnivale mask, teasing her with a riding crop. Plays it across her ass, flicks it against her crotch, then brings it down with a crack I can hear over the music hammering through the speakers.

The scent of the place is overwhelming. Alcohol, sex, the sharp sting of X and coke in the air. I can smell the fucking in the private rooms upstairs, the bathroom stalls in the back.

All that humanity. Meat and sweat. Easy to get overwhelmed. Dizzying. It makes me think of barbeque.

I shake it off. It doesn't take long to find Danny. He's tending bar in the back, chatting up the two girls Bruno let in, making them feel special, important. At heart he's a salesman. They don't realize they're the product.

His eyes flick to me as I step up behind them. He continues as though I'm not there. All smiles and free drinks. He says something to them, points at the woman who brought them over. They nod, excited, go off with her.

He looks at me, face changing. "About fucking time."

"I said I'd be here before you shut down. I'm here. You're not shut down. The fuck is the problem?"

To hell with him. I'm not here to dick around with Danny's little empire building scheme.

He leads me up a flight of metal stairs to the office. It's an impressive room. It should be. Simon shelled out a lot of cash for it. Enormous picture windows take in the whole club. Leather, wood, a billiard table, and walk-in humidor. Simon always had good taste. The place goes almost silent the moment the door closes, nothing but distant bass through the floor. The soundproofing alone must have cost a fortune.

Danny throws himself into a chair, sinks into it. Looks beat.

"You know how it happened?" he asks.

"Only what I heard on the news," I say. "Some cult thing. I don't buy it for a minute."

"Me either. That fucking Italian was there, right? Giavetti? I thought you were supposed to kill him."

"Would have, but he wasn't at his hotel. Spent all night trying to track him down. Must have tailed Simon from the house."

"I wish he'd had a bodyguard," Danny says in a tone that says exactly the opposite. "Well, there's fallout and shit's happening fast."

He gets up, paces the room. "I've had calls from everybody. Russians, Chinese, fucking Israelis. They've all heard about him. They're circling around like goddamn sharks."

Well, duh. Simon's death left a vacuum, and everyone wants to fill it. Sooner or later someone will.

Danny must be reading my mind. "I'm not gonna let 'em have it. Any of it."

"Simon's dead. They're gonna take it."

He waves me off, pulls a pack of Dunhills off a side table, and lights up. Doesn't offer me one.

"Just because Simon's gone doesn't mean the business is gone," he says. "You know how much of this thing I've been running. Simon was a fucking figurehead. And a retard. Wasn't for me this whole thing'd be in the shitter."

"So, you're the man now?"

"I am. And I've got a crew to make it stick."

"Then you don't need me," I say.

"The hell I don't," he says. "These guys are okay, but they're not like you. I need everyone to know that you're still a part of this. Your name carries a lot of weight. No reason why Simon kicking should leave you out in the cold."

I haven't seriously thought about working since the shit hit the fan. I've had higher priorities.

Speaking of which. "You mentioned somebody was asking about me."

"Huh? Oh, yeah. Some guy. Walking a midget."

"What, on a leash?"

"Yeah, actually. Thing kept sniffing the air like a fucking dog. Thought it was a gimp act. I don't handle that shit, man."

Weird, but I checked weird at the door a couple days ago and lost the ticket. "What'd he want?"

"Just that he wanted to talk to you about a stone. So, whatta ya say? You want the job, or not?"

"Give me some time to think about it."

Danny's not used to people saying no, or even maybe. His face twists into a sneer. "The fuck is there to think about? You want the job," he says. "You know it. You're useless if you don't have somebody to take orders from. Limited time offer. It's now, or walk."

He might not be used to people saying no, but I'm not used to ultimatums. Fuck him. "You think you know me? You know fuck all about me."

"Fuck you. You won't last the weekend without me," he says.

"Whatever. You have fun with those Israeli mobsters. I hear they like bolt cutters and nut sacks."

"You don't know the mistake you're making," he says.

Anger floods through me. "And you don't know who you're fucking with."

I could crack his sternum open, rip through his heart like I'm eating pulled pork. It's tempting. It'd shut the little fucker up. See if I can make his corpse dance for me.

I pull the impulse back, flashing back to the hooker and her pimp. That was different. It took me by surprise. This I want to do.

There are too many people downstairs. I don't want any piece of that fucker in my mouth.

I turn my back to him, open the door. House music floods the room, the bass hammers through me. I close the door on his temper tantrum and head downstairs.

I'm waiting for one of his bouncers to try to kick me out. I could use a fight right about now.

No one shows up.

So I do the next best thing; order an overpriced scotch at the bar.

Chapter 10

"You can't smoke in here," the bartender says. She wipes down the bar, puts down my fourth scotch.

I blow the smoke away from her. No reason to piss her off. She's just doing her job. Besides, I can smell the tobacco on her, see the cigarette tucked behind her ear.

"Yeah?"

"State law."

"You don't say."

She shakes her head, wipes her way back down the bar.

It's gotten quieter, the crowd less manic. Chilled out trance music floating out of the sound system. The floor show has taken on a subdued, almost reverent feel. The latest couple on stage are lost in each other, peeling pieces of leather from each other's bodies.

I sip my drink. I don't feel a thing. I wonder if it's even possible for me to get drunk anymore.

The bartender comes back, sets a drink in front of me that looks like a refugee from a Cabo resort; bright orange, reeks of tequila. Tall glass with fruit and an umbrella. I look up just to make sure she hasn't somehow turned into a cabana boy.

"The fuck is this?"

She points. "Lady at the table."

I look behind me. There's a girl in a booth raising her glass to me. Same fruity drink. She's got Veronica Lake hair, stunning eyes. Dressed less for a fetish scene and more for a cocktail party in shimmering blue. She stands out like a da Vinci on a coffee house wall.

And that screams of a setup.

I scan the crowd for anyone else who looks out of place. She's probably with the guy who's looking for me. Though having somebody who looks like her do the recon work seems a little odd. But I don't see anyone who doesn't belong. And certainly no guy with a midget on a leash.

"Didn't know this was that kind of place."

The bartender rolls her eyes. "It isn't," she says and goes to pour a beer for a guy slumped against the bar.

Well, whoever she is the blonde started this game. I raise my glass to her. She gets up from her booth and slides onto the bar stool next to me. Sticks out her hand. Not knowing what else to do, I shake it.

"Samantha Morgan." Her voice is like velvet.

"Joe Sunday."

"Buried yet?"

"Pardon?"

"Sorry." She stirs the ice in her glass with a long finger. I know she can't be for real, I mean I've got a good twenty-five years on her, but for a moment I'm tempted to suck the tequila off her fingertip. "It just reminds me of that poem. How does it go? 'Solomon Grundy, buried on Sunday?' Something like that?"

Oh. "No," I say. "Not yet, at least."

"Good. Above ground and out of jail. Can't ask for much more than that, can we?"

She sips at her drink looking at me over the rim of her glass. She's got gorgeous eyes. Blue, with flecks of slate in them.

"It's good to meet you, Joe. You seem so—" She pauses searching the air for a word. "Normal."

I can't help but laugh. "I'm so far from normal, I can't see it from here. But yeah, in this crowd, I suppose so." I realize she looks out of place, not because of the dress, but because she's seventy years too late. She should step out of an RKO picture, some black-and-white with William Powell. She gives off class like it's coming out her pores. Kind that makes a dozen men want to light her cigarette for her.

She lifts her glass, toasts the air in front of her. "To the appearance of normal. May it last forever." She sips her drink.

"So what brings you out here tonight?" she asks. "Tragedy or comedy?"

"Does it have to be either?"

"In my experience it usually is."

That one's easy. "I'd say tragedy."

"I'm sorry to hear that. The two aren't really all that different from each other, you know. All depends on whether the ending's happy."

"You don't say." I know she's linked with the stone somehow and what's happened to me, but there's something about her that sets me at ease.

"I think your problems could probably yield some pretty interesting opportunities," she says.

I'm sure you do. "Is this where you try to sell me on Amway?"

"Unitarianism, actually, but I can see you're not the cultish type. Besides, they kicked me out."

"Funny. I had the same problem with the Methodists."

I'd like to say this is the weirdest conversation I've had in a while, but the last twenty-four hours have been a lesson in freakish. Besides, she's so damn comfortable to talk to. It's easy, and fun. And for a few minutes, at least, I can forget about immortality and zombies and not breathing.

"What about you?" I ask. "What brings you out here?"

"Got bored, decided to check this place out. Nice vibe." She gives me that dazzling smile again. "Nice people."

"So you're not a regular?"

She shakes her head. "Oh, hell no. Though I must say I've been enjoying the show."

She seems to see my scotch for the first time. "If I'd known you were a serious drinker, I wouldn't be trying to ply you with this crap. What are you drinking?"

"Nothing." I slide the glass over to her. What's the point if you can't get drunk?

She reaches over, takes a sniff, a delicate taste.

"Oban. Pretty expensive nothing."

"You know your scotches. Consider it the obligatory drink I buy you."

"Obligatory? You make it sound like you're lancing a boil."

"If you don't want it." I start to pull the drink back, but her hand closes over mine. Her touch sends a ripple through me.

She keeps it there for a moment longer than is entirely comfortable, and her voice softens. "It's just what I'm in the mood for. Thank you." She looks at my hand. "You're awfully cold."

I'm not sure what to say to that, so I start to pull my hand away. "Sorry." I'm probably running right around room temperature. I'll have to figure out a way to hide that. Gloves?

She holds onto me. "No, it's nice. Soothing." She turns my hand palm up, stares at it with an odd intensity.

"Oh, now this is interesting," she says.

"My palm?"

"It's a window to the soul, you know. Same thing, really."

"Lot of pressure to put on a hand."

She turns it over, a jeweler examining a particularly rough diamond. Touches my fingertips, scarred knuckles. Carefully traces the crevices.

"You're a fighter. You've had some trouble with the law. See this line, here?" She runs a finger across a deep seam that runs the breadth of my hand. "Says you've got a long time ahead of you. But this one," she touches another near my thumb. "You die early."

"What else does my hand tell you?"

"That you have a thing for hot blondes who hit on you in fetish bars."

"You're good at this."

"It's a talent."

I suddenly realize how close she is, her scent strong, sweet. It cuts through the meaty sweat stink of the crowd. She smells like warm summers and lemonade, sunlight through the trees. And something a little darker below the surface.

I glance at my hand for signs of rot. But there's nothing. And this is a different feeling than the hooker. There was hunger there, blind need. But this is like melting in a hot tub. Relaxing.

But that's not something I have the luxury for anymore.

I pull my hand away. "You know," I say, "not to spoil the moment or anything, but I could be your dad."

"Not a chance," she says. "My dad was a bald cobbler who regularly beat his wife. You've got all your hair."

"That's not what I—" She shushes me with a finger to my lips. That touch again. She fills my vision until there's nothing but her and me. Even the music fades away.

The bartender sticks her head between us to tell us it's last call, and the spell breaks.

Samantha shivers, like she's just woken up. "And things were just getting interesting," she says. I look around, surprised to see how much the crowd has already thinned out.

"Lost some time there."

"Lost implies a waste," she says. "You know, I have a beautiful view from my apartment in Santa Monica. Care to see it?"

"Oh, now that depends," I say.

"On?"

"Whether you're a friend of Giavetti's or not."

The question hangs in the air between us, thick and heavy. A little pout on those luscious lips. Her eyes never leave mine.

"I was laying it on kind of thick, wasn't I?"

"Just a touch." I knew that it was all a show, but I'm still disappointed to find it confirmed. "So, I suppose you know Giavetti?"

"More or less. I hear you made him go away."

"Yeah? From who?"

"Oh, little birds here and there. You've stirred up quite a ruckus in the trees, you know."

"Don't suppose you want to elaborate?" I want to know what birds she's talking about and what trees. If I've got admirers, it'd be nice to know before they come after me.

"Maybe later." She pulls a brilliant white calling card from her handbag, hands it to me. *Samantha Morgan* and her phone number in florid script.

The change is abrupt. She's almost businesslike. "Just a second ago you were all for me coming home with you."

"Still am," she says, "but I think those gentlemen might have other ideas."

I turn my head. Big guy in a black suit and tie that, no matter how well tailored, isn't covering the fact that he could probably lift a boxcar. Buzz cut, pretty boy face. He could make it in movies if he weren't built like the poster boy for roid rage.

I didn't hear him come up behind me. Or smell him, for that matter.

He's holding something in his hand. Takes me a second to realize it's a leash. The midget on the other end pops his head out from behind his handler's tree-trunk legs.

Twisted body, rheumy eyes. But the resemblance to the giant holding him is unmistakable. Brothers? Father and son? They're even wearing the same suit.

I turn back and she's climbing off the barstool. Gives me a flash of thigh and that American sweetheart smile.

"Miss Morgan," the gorilla says, nodding his head at her.

"Archie," she replies. "Take care of yourself, Joe," she says to me. She leans in to kiss me on my cheek. Her lips close to my ear. "And don't believe everything you hear," she whispers. She steps away from the bar.

Not so fast. I'm not done with my questions. Maybe they're together. They obviously know each other. But the vibe is different. She doesn't like him. But she's not afraid of him, either.

I get up to block her path, and Archie is suddenly standing in front of me.

"Mr. Sunday," he says. "We need to talk."

"I'll get to you in a second," I say. I start to step around him, and the midget jerks in front of me and to the side, his leash pressing against my ankles. He snarls at me, showing needle-sharp teeth.

"I've been looking for you," Archie says.

I step over the leash, ready to punt the midget into next week. "So I've heard."

Samantha disappears between the curtains to the exit.

"Nothing sinister, I assure you," Archie says.

"All things considered, I doubt it." If I hurry I can get to her before she gets to the parking lot.

"You've eaten the heart of at least one person tonight, Mr. Sunday. Don't you think that's something worth discussing?"

That stops me dead. "What?"

"A heart," he says. "Some unfortunate stranger I hope. It would be a tragedy if your condition manifested itself around your loved ones."

"How do you know about that?"

"My employer," he says. "He's a doctor. He can help you. He's familiar with your condition."

"If you know so much, then you know I don't need a doctor."

"Mr. Sunday, tonight you were filled with a burning need you couldn't control. Do you think it's not going to happen again?"

"I was kinda hoping, yeah," I say.

"It's going to get worse," Archie says. "A lot worse. And soon. Come with me, and he can help you. Or don't, and you know what will happen. It's your choice. I really don't care either way."

My choice. Right.

Chapter 11

I shouldn't be surprised, but I am. The hell made me think this was going to be a free ride? I take a deep, empty breath.

"We can help you," Archie says. The midget behind him nods his head vigorously.

What the hell. It's not like he can make it worse. I follow them outside where they lead me over to a white Bentley in the club's parking lot. Leather trim, wood paneling.

Archie opens the back door for me. I start to get in and stop. "What's with the tarp in the back?"

"Sorry about that," Archie says, reaching past me to pull it out. "We weren't sure what condition you were going to be in when we found you."

I remember falling apart in that bathroom. How my hands turned gray, skin blistered and oozing yellow pus.

"Guess you weren't too worried about that new car smell." I edge past him, slide onto the seat.

As Archie drives, the midget peers at me over the top of the passenger seat. His skin is waxy, like it was carved from a block of resin. I resist the urge to go "Boo" at him. No telling what he'll do.

We cut west through Hollywood Boulevard, hookers and johns dotting the street corners, late night deals in front of the Chinese Theater.

"He have a name?"

Archie glances at me in the rearview. "Jughead," he says. Got to wonder what Betty and Veronica look like.

"I meant the doctor."

"Oh. Neumann. He's a good man. You'll like him. He can help you."

"So you keep saying. How exactly does he know me?"

He shrugs, Jughead aping his movements. They're weirdly in synch. "You'd have to ask him."

Jughead keeps staring at me. He's starting to creep me out.

"What's the deal with the midget? You brothers, or something?"

Archie laughs. "Or something. He's harmless. Unless I tell him not to be." Jughead smiles with that mouth full of lamprey teeth.

I file that away for later. Something tells me I'm going to need it.

———

The house, a three-story Spanish villa lit up like an airstrip, sits off of Mulholland, that winding spine of Los Angeles that slices the city in two. We hit a private road and enter the grounds through thick iron gates.

Archie and Jughead escort me through a massive oak door that looks like it was hauled over on a Spanish galleon, wrought iron gas torches on either side of it casting flickering yellow light.

The inside is an insane mash of art on every wall, every table. Banners in languages I don't recognize hang from the banisters. Latin inscriptions on plaques, Greek carved into tabletops. Playing cards are stuck in every doorjamb. The place has an oppressive feel. Like a castle or a prison.

"Nice place." If you're a fan of the Inquisition.

"The doctor likes it."

The midget, now off his leash, is watching me with wide-eyed wonder. Like a feral child.

"Does it talk?" I don't know where along the ride I stopped thinking of Jughead as "him." It's not a label that fits.

"No," Archie says.

Doctor Neumann is sitting at a reading table in a room that the word "library" simply can't do justice to. The room is two stories tall with shelves to the ceiling. Books, scrolls, notebooks jammed into every nook and overflowing. Ladders every ten feet.

Neumann's a tall guy with high cheekbones. Older. Maybe in his late fifties? Hard to tell. He's fit. Spry, I guess you'd call it. White hair, neatly trimmed goatee.

"Mr. Sunday," he says, all smiles. He stands up, crosses the room to grab my hand. Pumps it like he's pulling up oil. "I'm so glad they were able to find you. I was worried."

He looks me up and down. "I see. They found you too late, didn't they?" His face all grandfatherly concern. "I'm sorry for what's happened to you. It must have been awful."

"I've had better days."

"I'm sure you have. Please, sit down."

The room is full of chairs, but most of them are covered with maps and books. Thick sheaves of paper and rolled vellum cover every horizontal surface. The smell of old books and dust hangs heavy in the air.

He clears off a seat for me, dumping its contents heavily to the floor, then sweeps it all aside with a kick. I sit down, and he slides onto the corner of a desk.

"Archie here says you can help me," I say.

"Oh, indeed I can," he says. "But first, and please excuse my rudeness, but when was the last time you, ah, ate?"

"I had a burger yesterday."

"That's, ah, not quite what I meant."

"A few hours ago," I say. "I killed a whore in Hollywood."

He nods. "Good, good. Then we have some time. And time is important. You ate her heart, yes?"

That's good? "Yeah," I say. "Parts of some other stuff, too."

He looks thoughtful, considering something. "This is important," he says finally. "What did you do with the body?"

"I put a couple bullets into her brain after she started to chew on her pimp. Then I drove both of 'em to a gravel quarry and had them crushed into pulp."

He looks surprised. "Oh. Oh, yes, that would do it. Very creative. Very imaginative. That's an excellent sign."

"Okay, enough bullshit, Doc. It's an excellent sign of what? And can you help me or not?"

"Mr. Sunday, what do you know of your condition?"

"I get a bad rash and an irrational urge to eat prostitutes," I say. "And I'm dead."

"Yes, that's about the size of it," he says. "But there's more, obviously. I'm sure you know about the stone?" I nod. "Good, good. I'd always heard that Giavetti couldn't keep his mouth shut."

"You know him?" I break in.

"Know of him," he says. "By reputation. Now that stone, in case you hadn't figured this out already yourself, is the key to everything. It made you what you are, and you and the stone are linked, but it's not perfect. To stay this way, you need to feed. Do you see where this is going?"

"That's how you knew I'd eaten," I say. If they'd found me rotting this would probably be a pretty one-sided conversation. With a lot of "grr, argh," from me.

"Exactly. It was inevitable that you were going to kill someone tonight."

"So I just go around eating people, then, is that it?"

He laughs. "You could, I suppose. Or we could do something about it. I can restore what's been taken from you."

"Not sure I want to go back. Giavetti offered to make this stick. Didn't say anything about hearts but said he could make it without all the messy decomp." Which isn't that far from the truth, even if I didn't believe he could do it. "How about you, doc? Can you do that?"

"Yes," he says. "I can do that. But there's a catch."

"There always is."

"I can't do anything without the stone."

I fold my arms. I'm keenly aware of Archie and Jughead in the room, and if they haven't figured out where the stone is by now, they won't like what's about to happen. "Let me guess," I say. "You want me to find it."

"Exactly." There's a startled noise from Archie. "My normal means of acquiring it have so far failed. Since you and the stone have, shall we say, an intimate relationship with each other, I thought you might be more likely to locate it." He glares at Archie. "Not to mention more motivated."

"Sir," Archie says. "I don't think—"

"Did I ask you for your fucking opinion?" The kindly grandfather disintegrates only to reappear in an instant when he looks back to me.

"Knowing Giavetti he would have hidden the stone fairly well. Probably somewhere in that sanitarium he had you holed up in."

Neumann's already made up his mind about where the stone isn't, and I don't correct him.

"What do you say, Mr. Sunday. Would you be willing to find the stone so I can make you whole again?"

"Why do *you* want it?" I ask. If he knows what the stone can do, then he probably knows what Giavetti was trying to do with it.

"I think you know," he says, smiling.

I make a show of thinking about it.

"How do I know you can do it?"

He cocks his head to one side, thinking. "About five years ago," he says, "a book came up for auction in China. It was a set of German research notes from World War II. The stone was held by the Third Reich until the fall of Berlin when it disappeared."

"That's nice." I pull my cigarettes out of my jacket. I don't see a no smoking sign, and I wouldn't care if I did. But I left my lighter in my car, and I don't see any matches.

"Allow me," Neumann says. Flames appear over his fingertips, and he leans forward to light my Marlboro.

"Neat trick."

"It has its uses. The Germans were trying to understand the stone by experimenting on hundreds of Jewish prisoners. None of them were what you would call a complete success."

Jesus. Auschwitz must have been a walk in the park to what those poor fuckers went through. "And you have the book?"

"No. I understand Giavetti purchased it. I rescinded my bid. I had an opportunity to inspect it and realized quickly that it was a fake. An excellent forgery, mind, but missing quite a lot of crucial information. Better to not have it at all than to try to follow its instructions."

"How do you know that?" I ask, already guessing at the answer and not liking it one goddamn bit.

"Because I wrote it."

He doesn't look old enough, but that doesn't mean much in this crowd. I take a deep drag off my cigarette, blow the smoke directly in his face. He doesn't cough.

"You're one evil fucking bastard," I say.

"So I've been told. The point of this story is that I know how to use that stone far better than Giavetti ever could. In fact, if he's planning on doing with it what I think he is, he'll end up in even worse shape than you."

That puts a new spin on things. Is Giavetti being set up? The more I think about it the more I realize I don't know what the hell is going on.

"That's about all I can offer as credentials. But I do know that when I was experimenting with the stone, I got almost as far as Giavetti did with you. Unlike him, though, I also managed to reverse it in a few cases. Those subjects who weren't so far gone that they couldn't reason, for example."

"That why you think it was good that I was imaginative in getting rid of my corpses?"

"Yes," he says. "It makes the possibility of bringing you back or of, as you put it, 'making it stick' that much easier. I have to admit a grudging respect for Giavetti's handiwork. Now, do we have a deal?"

"Yeah," I say. "It's a deal." I don't see how this would work out any different than if I'd agreed with Giavetti. There's no proof that Neumann won't just bring me back and kill me again, but I'll burn that bridge when I get to it.

"Good." He scribbles a number on a notepad, tears out the page to hand to me. "You can reach me at this number. I'll want to keep updated." He turns to Archie, still fuming at his replacement. "Take Mr. Sunday back. Safely."

Archie stalks out of the room, Jughead close at his heels. The midget throws a glare over his shoulder then disappears through the door.

"One last question, Doc," I say. "How long do I have?"

"Before you need to feed? About a day."

A day? "You're fucking kidding me. That's it?"

"That's how it was in the camps. Some lasted longer than others. You'd be amazed how many Jews someone like you could go through in a week. And the emotional toll. Aren't you glad you didn't kill anyone close to you?"

I used to think Evil existed. Now, I wonder if I'm looking right at it. I turn away, not answering him.

He calls to me as I step through the library door. "Be careful, Mr. Sunday. I know I don't have to tell you that you're running on borrowed time. The sooner you get me the stone, the sooner we can fix this problem for you."

———

The drive back is faster. It's about four a.m. and the sun is still a couple hours off.

"Interesting guy, the Doc," I say. "You like working for him?"

Archie looks at me in the rearview mirror. I can feel him seething in the front seat.

"I do," Archie says finally. "I owe him a great debt. We all do."

"All?" Something tells me he's not talking about the midget.

"I'm not the only one who works for Doctor Neumann. He's very well known in certain circles."

"I'd never heard of him. Guess I don't run in those certain circles."

"Undoubtedly. L.A.'s a big place, Mr. Sunday. There's more than just gangbangers, porn, and ingénues. A lot more."

"'More in heaven and earth than are dreamt of in your philosophy'?"

"Exactly. I wouldn't have taken you for a Shakespeare fan."

"Is that what it's from? Heard it in a movie once."

So Neumann's a big fish. How big is the pond? And what kind of sharks are swimming in it?

———

I know something's wrong the moment I see my front door. It's closed, but the jamb is broken. My porch light is out. The door swings open at my touch.

I step inside and flick the light switch. The lamp's been knocked to the floor, casting eerie shadows through the room.

Whoever broke in did a thorough job. Cushions are sliced open, stuffing on the floor. Books in a pile, pictures off the wall.

I rush to the bedroom closet, throw it open. The safe's sitting wide open. Nothing's missing, not the cash, not the guns.

Nothing except the stone.

Chapter 12

I sift for half an hour before giving up. It's not here. Neumann said I've got some kind of link to it. Maybe if I close my eyes and wish really hard, it'll call my name or something.

I try it. No such luck.

What do I know? I'm starting to panic. I can tell because I'm pacing. I only pace when I'm starting to lose it. I force myself to stop moving and think.

Wherever it is, I'm not going to find it standing in a pile of busted CDs and overturned furniture. I start righting things, sift through piles of books and tossed through clothes.

The light outside my window goes from black to gray. I clean the house up best I can, but the thief did such a thorough rollover, the place looks like hell no matter what I do.

By the time I've got things at least livable, the sun's poking over the palm trees.

As I'm sorting through a pile of random crap, I find something I know I've never had before. It's a broken piece of a blue card. Like a credit card, but a hole punched in one corner and the words LA COUNTY DE in raised letters. A library card? I pocket it, not sure what to do with it.

So, how do I find the stone? I don't know where to start.

The best person I know at finding stuff out is Carl. But after our fight in the gym I doubt he'll talk to me.

Besides, he'll want to know why I'm looking. What happened to my house. What happened last night. I can't pull him into this. He's my friend. Was my friend, at least. Now, I don't know.

I push the thought aside. Focus. People, I know how to find. You ask a bunch of questions, break some fingers. Go to the last place they were seen.

That gives me an idea.

I find my toppled computer. It's dented, and the side's been torn off, but other than that it works fine. I run a quick internet search on the burglary in Bel Air that started this whole mess.

In a few minutes I have the name of the guy who owned the stone, Kyle Henderson, and his address.

Henderson took a bullet during the burglary. Went into Emergency with a sucking chest wound, went out in a body bag. He hung on long enough to tell the cops that it was three guys and was able to give a description of one of them.

The police have thoroughly gone over the place. I don't doubt that. I don't know if he was married, had children, or anything else about him. If I'm lucky maybe I can get someone to talk to me, maybe a neighbor. See if maybe there's something anyone might not have asked.

Of course, Bel Air people don't usually talk to folks like me. Roughing up a rich soccer mom with private security a minute away doesn't appeal, but I'll figure something out.

With a place to start, my mind calms down enough to think about things a little. Who'd want the stone? Anybody who knew about it, that's who. And that list keeps getting longer. Neumann, Giavetti, Frank. I look over the card Samantha gave me, wonder what her role is in all this.

No time like the present. I wonder if she's an early riser. I dial the phone, get her voice mail.

Before I can leave a message someone starts hammering on my front door.

I hang up, pull the Glock.

I smell him before I get there, but I don't need to do that to know who it is. I know that knock. It's a cop knock.

"Goddamn you wear a lot of aftershave," I say, opening the door. Frank looks like shit. I doubt he's slept much. "Is that the same suit you were wearing last night?"

"Fuck you," he says, elbowing his way in. He looks at the gun in my hand, ignores it. He's got a pair of Samsonites under his eyes, hasn't shaved. I'm wondering if the reality of what's going on is finally sinking in, and he can't handle it. I don't blame him. I keep wondering when it's going to really hit me.

"By all means, come on in."

"I don't have time to— The fuck happened in here?" He's in shock, looking at the shambles of my living room like he's never seen a burglary before.

"Wild night. What can I do for you, Detective?"

"We're going to the morgue."

"Thanks, but I already have a place to stay."

"It's Giavetti."

"Yeah?" I say. "He finally walk out of there?"

"Dunno," he says. "Somebody sure as hell did."

———

The main morgue for L.A. County is across the river on Mission. It's a sad little neighborhood. Everything covered in a fine layer of gray from the nearby rail tracks and the car smog from the 5 Freeway. I can see the sun rising hazily over the city as we wend our way through early morning traffic.

"I thought you kept regular hours," I say. "Why so early?"

"Not like the morgue closes."

"No, but you do."

"Since when do you worry about me?"

"Since you're the one who's keeping me out of the massacre at Giavetti's."

"Yeah, well you don't have to worry about that anymore. The place burned down last night. Any evidence you might have been there went up with it."

"Accident?"

"What do you think?"

"Any leads?"

He glances over at me, his cop stare coming out for just a second. "Besides you? Where'd you go last night, anyway?"

"Out. How about you, Detective? Giving B&E a try? Looking for a new career?"

"Like you've got anything I want. I got better things to do than roll your place, Sunday."

The back and forth is just going to piss us both off, so I drop it. "So what happened at the morgue?"

"Got a call from a guy I know over there. Owes me for not busting his ass on a narcotics charge. I asked him to keep an eye out for anything weird and let me know soon as it happens. I dropped some cash to have him go over the nightly security tapes. Thinks he's got something."

"Anybody else know?"

"Shouldn't. He's too freaked out to talk about it."

We pull into the parking lot and slide into a space reserved for police officers. The morgue has been here for a long time, white facade and redbrick all around. Never been in myself. Always figured when I popped by, it'd be in a bag.

"They do the autopsy yet?"

"Doubt it. They're backlogged over a week. Goddamn mess. Corpses stacked on corpses. Three to a drawer on a bad day."

We go in. Disinfectant, heavy stink of days-old rot, cut open bodies. I'd fit right in.

Air fresheners in random corners of the lobby add a nice floral tinge. It might help, but with my newly sensitive nose it just smells like somebody shit on a rosebush.

Frank flashes his badge and signs us in. The receptionist hands us ID badges.

"We're here to see DeWalt."

The receptionist makes a call, and a nervous looking guy in surgical scrubs comes out a minute later. He's got a haggard look, bloodhound jowls.

"Frank," he says, eyeing me suspiciously. I don't look like a cop. I just don't give off that vibe. Then again, this guy's been around cadavers so long, maybe I'm tipping his radar.

"This is Detective Battles," Frank says pointing at me. "He's cool." DeWalt calms down instantly.

He takes us into one of the refrigerator rooms. The place is all cold steel and ceramic tile. Noticeably rank. There's a small desk and computer crammed over to the side. He's talking in a low whisper. God knows why, nobody back here but him, Frank, and dead people.

"So, I'm checking last night's tapes and around one a.m., I get this." He brings up the video on his computer. It's the hallway we just came through.

Nothing for a second. Then a naked man, old and withered, hobbles out of the refrigeration room, crosses over to another room. It's hard to tell if it's Giavetti, because his face is turned away from the camera.

DeWalt fast-forwards the video. "That's the locker room he went into. He comes out about twenty minutes later." Sure enough, he hobbles back out, but now he's got surgical scrubs and a lab coat. He turns and heads toward the front door, and that's when we catch his face.

It's Giavetti all right.

"Fuck me," Frank says.

"Is this what you were looking for?" DeWalt asks. "This guy hide in a bag and come in or something?" He's reaching and he knows it, but the alternative doesn't bear thinking about.

"Yeah," Frank says. "Yeah, it's what we're looking for. Anybody sign out last night around then?"

"Nope. Camera caught him leaving, though. Walked right past the night receptionist like she didn't even see him."

"Probably didn't," I say. Frank gives me a look telling me he'd rather DeWalt stayed in the dark.

"Okay. Can you crack open one of these drawers?"

DeWalt hesitates. "This is just some guy hopped a ride on a morgue wagon, right?"

"Yeah," Frank says. "Just some psycho. Probably came in to fuck an overdose or something. Good thing you brought this to me."

DeWalt's nodding. Necrophilia's something he can understand. "Yeah. Just some psycho," he says. "So, what drawer you're looking for?"

"Guy came in yesterday morning from that shootout up in the hills."

DeWalt winces. "He's not one of the messed up ones, is he? Most of them are still double bagged to keep them in one piece."

"GSW to the skull."

"Oh, the headshot? Yeah he's right here. We had to double them up. He's in here with a multiple stab wound."

DeWalt starts to slide open a drawer. Frank stops him.

"Why don't you go and get some coffee, okay?" he says.

DeWalt looks from Frank to me and back again. "You sure?"

"Yeah. We'll let you know if we need anything."

DeWalt leaves, anxiously looking over his shoulder at us. Frank closes the door behind him.

I slide the drawer open, unzip the body bag.

"This isn't Giavetti," I say. "I'm not even sure it's a person."

"The fuck are you talking about?" he says, coming over to me. I step aside to give him a good look.

"Fuck me," he says.

The body looks like it was pulled from the pyramids at Giza. It's nothing but a mummy dressed in a Lakers T-shirt and jeans that are now five sizes too big. The skin is tight and dried out, bones poking through the stab wounds. I'd swear he was a hundred years old before he died. The toe tag says he's nineteen.

There's a list on the inside of the drawer, an extra body bag underneath.

"DeWalt said he was double drawered. So this is the second guy," I say.

"Christ, what happened to him?"

I pull the drawer next to Giavetti's, unzip the bag. A woman. Same thing.

"Same thing that happened to this one," I say.

I pull more drawers open, check bodies. All of the ones around Giavetti's drawer are in the same condition. Mummies. They're all the same up to three bodies away from where he was stored. Some of them are more dried out than others.

"How did he do this?" Frank says.

I shrug. "Fuck if I know. Sucked 'em dry, maybe? Pulls out fluids like a vampire?"

"That's disgusting," Frank says. I agree. The human body's got some pretty vile things in it. I should know, I oozed a lot of them out last night.

"Maybe it's something else. All of these were brought in within a day after he was. Maybe there was some, fuck, I dunno, *life* left in 'em? Maybe he pulled it out of them? Used it on himself?"

"That's insane."

"You got a better idea? It's not like he walked out of here with half his head missing."

Frank looks at the open drawers, the mummified corpses. "I need a cigarette," he says, walks out the door.

———

It explains a lot, but Frank's still having trouble with it. Hell, I'm having trouble with it. Dead's dead. You'd think he'd need a live body to pull some kind of vampire schtick. But the hell do I know? Maybe he just needs meat.

We're smoking out back near the loading dock, a couple of morgue wagons sitting ready to go out at a moment's notice.

"So, he dies, but he doesn't really die. And then he finds another body and pulls shit out of it?" Frank says.

"Well, he's always looked the same, right?"

"Yeah. Jesus. I thought . . ." He lets the sentence fade to nothing.

He thought that this was all really a nightmare, I'm thinking.

I looked at Frank. "You haven't slept much, have you?"

"That obvious?"

"Just a little. Nightmares?"

"Yeah. Man, you saw what he did to those people. You know what he did to you. Of course, I'm having fucking nightmares. Aren't you?"

"I don't sleep anymore."

He shakes his head, the look on his face disgust or exasperation. I'm not sure which. "There," he says. "That right there. That's what I'm talking about. You don't sleep anymore. You don't breathe. The fuck are you?"

"You think I don't ask myself that same question every five minutes?"

"Yeah, but you're so goddamn accepting of all this. Why you and not Julio? Why not those others Giavetti tried to change? You just seem to roll with it."

I grind the butt of my cigarette under my heel, pull a fresh one from a pack.

"Maybe that's it," I say. "Maybe I'm, I dunno, more resilient?"

"More stupid, maybe."

That was going to be my next choice. But I think I'm onto something there. Julio was a good guy, but he just couldn't handle change. Me, hell, I'm an L.A. boy. Change is our chief export. You want to reinvent yourself, come to this town.

I think that's it. Yeah, stuff gets to me, but mostly none of it fucking matters. It is what it is, you know? Lose an eye, big fucking deal. You've got another one. Shit happens.

We redefine normal like nobody's business out here. You accept it and move on.

Of course, I have to admit, being dead sort of stretches that one a bit.

I change the subject. "So, Giavetti's out. What now?"

"I'll put a BOLO out on him. He's bound to pop up somewhere. I might be able to get some tapes of the area. ATMs, security cameras, that kind of thing. I gotta wonder where he'd have headed."

I remember the piece of blue plastic card I found earlier. I pull it from my pocket. Looking at the damn thing for the last couple hours, I should have made the connection earlier. My mind fills in the gaps of the letters on the back. Put them all together and they spell out LA DEPART-MENT OF CORONER.

"What's that?" Frank asks.

"Part of a toe tag," I say. I know exactly where Giavetti headed when he left the morgue. I do the math. He would have had plenty of time to get to my place, ransack the shit out of it, and walk off with the stone.

And he left the tag as a souvenir. But where'd he go after that?

"I don't even want to know why you have that," he says. He stubs out his cigarette, rubs a hand over his haggard face. "Jesus. You should be in there wearing that thing and stuffed in a body bag, not out here walking and talking."

"Well, I am," I say, "so get used to it."

"No. That I won't do. I don't know what the fuck you are, but I am not going to getting used to you." He starts toward his car, shows me a hand when I follow him. "Find your own ride home. I'm fucking done here."

"Gee, thanks, detective. And I thought we were getting to be friends."

He gives me the finger, slides behind the wheel of his Crown Vic. Bastard.

To be honest, I can't blame him. I'm not sure I'll get used to me, either.

Chapter 13

I pull out my phone to call a cab and see the little flashing light of a missed call. Samantha's number. It must have rung while I was in the morgue, but the heavy brick and metal drawers swallowed the signal.

I dial her back. It rings four times before it goes to voice mail— Samantha's voice on the other end telling me to leave a message.

"Hey," I say when the machine beeps. "This is Joe. Thought you might want to know Giavetti's out of the morgue." She picks up with a speed that says panic, and a voice that says anything but. I'm not sure which one to believe.

"Joe," she says. "So nice to hear from you. How are you doing?"

"Not bad. All things considered."

"You say Sandro's up and about?"

"Yeah, last night. You sound surprised."

"A little. He's usually much quicker about that sort of thing. Especially if he's in a morgue. How was your meeting with Doctor Neumann? I assume that's where Archie and his friend took you?"

Much quicker about that sort of thing? I'm sure he is. He's probably had a lot of practice.

"Well enough," I say. "I'd like to see you some time. I think we have a lot to talk about."

"I'm sure we do," she says. "Any idea where Sandro is now?"

"Funny, I thought you might be able to tell me."

She laughs. "Hardly. If he confides in anyone anymore, it's not likely to be me."

"Sounds like you two had a falling out."

"It was a long time ago. Now, did you just call to tell me Sandro was running around again, or did you have something else in mind?"

"Well, you know, that was just an excuse."

"An ulterior motive, Mr. Sunday? I'm shocked. Whatever happened to 'I was just in your neighborhood'?"

"That only works if I know where your neighborhood is." I pull the card she gave me from my pocket. No address. But a bit of the conversation from last night sticks in my memory. "Santa Monica's a big place, after all."

"Oh, please," she says. "It's not that big. A resourceful man such as yourself, I'm surprised you haven't shown up on my doorstep yet."

"I'm a little surprised you haven't shown up on *my* doorstep," I say.

"That would be showing a little too much interest, don't you think? Besides, I don't stalk a man's house until at least the third date. And only if he's married."

"Guess I'll never come home to find you sitting on my couch, then?"

"Do you have a couch?" she says. "You don't strike me as the type."

"I'm funny that way. I even wear matching socks and clean underwear. You should see it sometime."

"The couch?"

"The underwear."

"I may have to take you up on that. In the meantime, why don't I help you out a little? I'm near Wilshire and Ocean. I'm sure you can figure out the rest. Come on over when you have time."

"Is this your idea of hard to get?"

"If I were hard to get I'd be in Paris by now. No, I just like a man who's not afraid to show his intelligence. I'll see you later? Tonight, maybe?"

"Maybe."

"Until then." She hangs up with a click.

So she and Giavetti had a falling out. Don't get along. So, why's she so eager to find out where he is? Is she afraid of him?

Women. They can never fucking make it easy.

———

Knowing that Giavetti's up and about doesn't change much. I still don't have anything to go on to find him. The Bel Air address is the only lead I've got, and that's iffy at best.

Bel Air's not my usual stomping ground. These aren't mansions, they're compounds. A-Listers, big time producers, moguls. If you take a deep breath you can smell the cash.

Which means nobody in their right mind is going to talk to me.

When Giavetti broke into my safe he wasn't exactly subtle. The outside hinges are scratched all to hell, and the dial was ripped out the front. He had a crowbar, a lot of patience, and even more motivation. My safe didn't stand a chance.

I pull off the duct tape I've secured it with and rummage through the back until I find a black plastic case with a couple of fake LAPD badges in it. I grab one and clip it onto my belt.

It won't stand up to too much scrutiny, and I don't need to use it often. Sometimes, though, a badge can help get me into places I might not normally be able to.

I take the canyon roads above UCLA past the Bel Air Country Club into the winding streets north of Sunset. My car's not the greatest, but it's not as if anything I could afford would ever fit in this neighborhood.

The house is a sprawling mansion complex with a Sotheby's Real Estate sign out front. The man's been dead what, a week? Guess money buys speed.

I pull up outside the gates behind a Mexican dragging a lawnmower out of the back of a beat-up Chevy truck.

"Hey," I say, "You work on this house here?"

He looks at me, confused. Maybe doesn't speak English.

I flash him the badge, say "¿Usted trabajan aquí?" in broken Spanish.

He laughs. "Man, you really need to work on that accent. I heard you the first time. Yeah, I'm working here. What do ya need?"

"You work the house for long?"

He shakes his head. "Nah. The realtor brought me in to clean up the grounds. I got three other guys already inside."

"So you never been here before?"

"Yesterday was our first time. Hey, I hear the guy lived here got killed. That true?"

"Yeah. Burglary."

He gives a low whistle. "Damn. That was stupid."

"How do you mean?"

"I heard the guy had security cameras, dogs. Alarms comin' out his ass. I've got like, ten codes I gotta put in just to get into one of the backyards."

And three bozos waltzed in and snagged the stone?

"Yeah," I say. "We're still looking into it. They showing the house yet?"

"No. Got cleaners inside, though. Driveway's overloaded." He kicks his tires. "That's why I got this piece of shit parked out here."

"Thanks."

I head inside, leaving him to struggle with his equipment. I walk through the open gates onto a sea of cars parked in front of a place that looks more like Versailles than Los Angeles.

Did he live alone? Wife? Girlfriend? At the least there should be a maid or two. I head up the enormous staircase, looking for anyone who looks like they might be more than temporary help.

A thick man in a Tommy Bahama shirt, silk pants, and a tan the color of old wood steps out of the door as I'm coming up the front stairs. He smiles with teeth so white I'm glad I'm wearing sunglasses.

"Peter Lippscomb, Sotheby's Realty. Sorry, but the house isn't ready to be seen yet."

"That's okay, Peter." I flash him the badge. "I'm not here to buy." His face falls as he leans in to see it. I pull it back before he can get a good look at it.

"Oh. Uh, what can I do for you, officer—?"

"Detective," I say.

He blinks at me, waiting for a name. I don't give him one. "Oh," he says. "This is about Mr. Henderson isn't it?"

"I'm just following up on some things. Getting some paperwork closed out. Did you know him?"

"No. I never met him. Never heard of him before Sotheby's brought me in, in fact. I think some of the cleaning crew worked here before— well, before."

"If I could talk to one or two of them, that'd really help me out. Paperwork, you know." He nods knowingly, like he cares.

He leads me inside through a pair of wrought iron and glass front doors. One side has a board where the glass should be.

"We're getting that fixed," Peter says. "I guess it got shot out or something? I'm really not sure."

There's a guy waxing the marble floor in the foyer, someone else dusting the banister of the enormous staircase. The walls have been stripped bare, but there are patches where pictures were taken down. Considering the general gaudiness of the place, they could have been dogs playing poker as easily as *Blue Boy*.

"Was the owner married? Have any kids?"

"I know he wasn't married, but I don't know about kids. I think he pretty much had this whole place to himself."

"Lot of space for one guy."

"Yeah. Thank god for the rich. Guys like him keep me employed."

"Does a place usually move so quickly? Figured it would still be in probate."

He nods. "It would be. If he'd owned it."

"He rented?"

"Not quite. I'm not really sure what the arrangement was. It's owned by Imperial Enterprises. Again, I'm not sure what they do. Importing? Maybe high tech?" He shrugs.

He takes me on a tour through the bottom floor. The bathrooms are bigger than some apartments I've had. We find a woman cleaning windowsills in a guest bedroom.

"Angie," he says. "Were you working here when Mr. Henderson was living here?"

She nods. A small woman, purple hair with brown roots and a ring through her nose. Nineteen? Twenty? Her eyes look as if they've seen a lot more.

"Yeah. Me and a few others. Why?"

"Hi, Angie," I say. "I'm with the LAPD. I was wondering if I could talk to you about something." I pull out my little cop notebook and a pen, try to look official.

"I didn't steal anything." She's got the look of the accused. Like she's been hammered for ripping off people that she never touched, never thought about touching.

"Didn't think you did," I say. I remember being her age. Getting grilled by some fat fuck who thought he could mess with me just because I was young, or had a leather jacket, or a skateboard, or long hair.

"I just wanted to ask you a few things about Mr. Henderson. Nothing's gone missing, and I'm not here to talk about anything being stolen."

She narrows her eyes, not trusting me. "Okay," she says.

"Were you here the night of the break-in?"

She shakes her head. "No. I left a couple hours before then. Nobody was home."

"Do you know if he had people over a lot? Girlfriend? Boyfriend?"

She pauses. Trying to think. There's something there. "Yeah," she says, stretching out the word like taffy. "There was someone. But I—I don't remember who."

I don't get the vibe that she's lying. Her face is turning a little red, like she's thinking through a migraine.

"Don't hurt yourself," I say. That seems to calm her down.

"I don't know why I can't remember," she says.

"You remember anything at all? Man? Woman? Short? Tall?"

"Yeah. I know I do. I just . . . It was a man. No. A woman?" She shrugs. "Sorry." I wonder if Frank had this problem. Probably.

"Do you know anyone else who worked here at the time?"

I talk to three people. Two women and a man who worked the yard. Calling it an interview is a bit of a stretch, though. If they remember anything they contradict themselves and each other. Same look on their faces like every time they remember, it hurts.

I leave Peter at the front gate. Somebody was here, and nobody remembers who?

More questions than answers. Somebody went to a lot of trouble to make it that way.

Chapter 14

Normally, I hit a brick wall, I'd hash things out with Julio, and we'd come up with what to do next. Not really an option anymore now, is it?

I knew that one of these days somebody was going to punch one of our tickets. Always thought I'd be the first one to go. And a little more conventionally.

I push the thought away. Getting maudlin's going to do fuck-all for my problems.

What I need is perspective. The only person left I can think of I might get that from probably doesn't want to talk to me.

Well, fuck it. Not much choice. I dial Carl, hoping he hasn't shut off his phone. He usually turns off the ringer when he's at the paper.

I have a lot of apologizing to do. And, shit, I'll have to tell him what's going on. Not sure how he'll handle it. Can I trust him not to lose his mind?

The phone rings four times before voice mail picks it up. I start to leave a message then hang up before I say anything. What the hell do I tell him? Give him the real story or feed him some bullshit and hope he doesn't see through it?

If I tell him the truth he's either going to think I'm insane or just fucking with him. And then there's how much truth. Sure, he knows I'm hired muscle. He knows the kinds of circles I run in. Hell, I've been feeding him scraps for the news for years now.

He said he knows what I really do, but does he? The killings or was that just an educated guess? That's one thing I haven't been willing to tell him about.

But I've known him most of my life. He's my friend. Probably the only one I have left, in fact. Christ, I'm glad my parents are already dead. Imagine going to your mom with a story like this.

It's going to have to be the truth. All of it. I need more than just per-spective. I need somebody I can rely on. And that depends on trust.

I call him again, expecting the same tinny voice telling me to leave a message.

Instead I get screaming.

"Carl?" I say, trying to push my voice over the noise coming through the phone.

"Help me," he says in a voice like sandpaper. "Joe, please. Please, please. I need help."

"What the hell is going on? Where are you?"

His voice descends to a whisper. "I fucked up," he says. "I'm sorry, man. God, I'm sorry. Should have listened. Should have listened to you. Fucked up. Fuckedupfuckedupfuckedup."

"Carl, I need you to calm down and tell me what you did. What's happening?"

"You told me. Told me to drop it. Leave it alone."

Shit. He did what any reporter would do. He dug. And I can only imagine what he found when the hole got deep enough.

"Carl, listen to me very carefully. I need to know this. Are you still breathing?"

That stops him. "What?" he says.

"Are you still alive?"

"The fuck? Of course I'm still alive. I need help, goddammit. I need, fuck I don't what I . . . I need. . . ." His voice trails off. "Who is this?"

"It's Joe," I say, my momentary relief that he's not like me dissolving into a new worry. "You said you're in trouble."

"Joe? I fucked up, man," he says. "I should have listened."

"Yeah, we covered that." I can't keep having this conversation with him. I won't get anything useful out of him over the phone. "Where are you?"

"Uh . . . I'm in a hotel room. Yeah." I hear stumbling, a drawer open-ing. "I'm at a Marriott. I think it's the one by the airport." He rattles off an address, gives me a room number on the fifth floor. "Why am I here, Joe? What happened to me? I can't remember."

"Hang tight," I say. "I'll be there as soon as I can."

Afternoon traffic down to the airport sucks. An hour goes by before I pull into the hotel's parking garage.

The hotel's lobby is spacious, done in soft yellows and deep reds. It's got the generic feel of a shopping mall. As if you could step outside and be in Nashville or Newark just as easily as you could be in Los Angeles.

I hurry to the fifth floor, slowing myself down so as not to draw attention. The hallway is deserted, anonymous doors stretching into the distance.

Carl's room is shoved into a corner, a DO NOT DISTURB tag hanging from the doorknob. I knock.

"Carl," I say, head next to the door, voice low. Never know who else might be in the room next door. "It's Joe. Let me in."

He pulls the door open a crack, only as far as the security stop will let it go. His face is hard to make out in the darkness of the room. He has the shades drawn.

"Joe?" he whispers. "That you?"

"Yeah, Carl, it's me. Let me in."

"No," he says. "She's trying to trick me again. It's not you."

"Who's tricking you, Carl?"

"Some guy," he says, distracted. "No. Some woman? Joe, is that you?" His face presses against the crack in the doorway to get a better look at me, and I step back in alarm.

It's Carl, but not the Carl I know. His face looks like he's been on the street for the last ten years. Drawn and weathered. He's lost a lot of weight. He has a pillowcase wrapped around his skull and low on his forehead, like a bald cancer patient.

"It's me," I say.

Fear, confusion, and terror in those eyes. He reaches fingers through the door, and I take them in my hand. Tears are streaming down his face.

"Let me in, Carl," I say. "Let me in, and I'll take care of you."

———

Carl's been babbling for half an hour in the darkened room. I turned on a light, but he started screaming. His speech is disjointed. Events don't flow one into the other but jump around like a spastic grasshopper. Like somebody broke him into a thousand pieces and then glued them back together in the wrong order.

Eventually I piece together that after our fight the other day he went looking into what happened to Simon and all those corpses they pulled out of the canyon. Burned the midnight oil, pulled some leads together in record time. He was going to meet someone and then—

And that's all he can remember before finding himself in this room. He has no idea who he was going to talk to. If it was a man or a woman. When he tries to remember I can see the pain in his eyes, like he's fighting through a migraine. I know that look. It's the same look the housekeepers in Bel Air had trying to remember who else had been at the mansion.

"And then I was here," he says. He's lucid at the moment. But he's been lucid four times in the last thirty minutes and I know it won't last. "I tried to leave, but I can't."

I look at the door. Nothing keeping him in. Nothing kept me out. "How come?"

"It hurts," he says simply.

"Like the headaches?"

He shakes his head. "No. That's nothing. Like I'm on fire. Deep down into my soul. Never felt so much pain before. Every time I try to walk out that door."

"What if I carried you through?"

His eyes go wide, and he shakes his head. "No. God, no. They tried that when they came for me. I screamed, and they hit me. Kept hitting me. Hurt less to be hit."

"Whoa, back up," I say. "Who is this? Somebody came here before I did?" I check to make sure the security stop is back in place, check through the peephole.

Carl laughs. "They're not out there," he says. "They don't need to be." He touches the pillowcase wrapped around his forehead. "Two guys and a child. Came by this morning. Kid looked like he was raised by wolves. Had him on a leash."

"Was one of the guys about my size? Other one old?"

"Yeah. You know them."

"Old guy's named Neumann. The others are Archie and Jughead," I say. Carl must have gotten close enough to what was going on to grab Neumann's attention, and they tracked him down here.

I pick up Carl's emaciated wrist. He must have lost thirty pounds and gained thirty years in the last day. "Did they do this to you?" I ask.

He shakes his head. "I was like that when I came to in here. They just asked me questions. Wondering who I was, what I was doing. When I didn't give them what they wanted the old guy said he'd keep an eye on me." He barks out a laugh. The craziness in that one sound chills my spine. It lingers in the air for too long.

"They ask about me?" I say.

Carl looks startled. "No," he says. "Why would they do that?"

"No reason. What'd you tell them?"

"Just what I told you," he says. "That I was looking into that murder in the Santa Monica Mountains and then I woke up here. Why'd they come here, Joe? Why'd they want to know?" He starts to rock back and forth in his seat.

It's a child's question. I know this lucid period is over, but I need more information.

"I need you to focus," I say. "Did they do anything else? Ask anything else?"

He stares at me, and I know he doesn't remember who I am. He points to the pillowcase on his head. I untie the knot in the back and lift it off.

A single, oversized blue eye sits in the middle of his forehead. I stare at it. It stares at me. I blink first.

Neumann did say he'd keep an eye on him.

I put the pillowcase back over his forehead and cinch it up tight.

Carl starts to babble some more. Wanting his mommy, asking for ice cream.

I don't know what to do. Try to take him out of the room? Get him really drunk, knock him out, and drag him downstairs? And what happens when he wakes up? Would that even work?

His babbling is becoming more incoherent. Numbers and random words. He starts repeating himself. And then I realize he's saying an address.

I grab a pen and paper from the nightstand and write down what he's saying. I'm not sure, but it looks like it's somewhere downtown.

"What is this, Carl?" I say. But all I get out of him is more of his *Rain Man* impression.

I listen some more but nothing else makes any sense. Finally, I can't stay any longer.

"I have to go," I say. "Sit tight. I'll figure something out." I open the door to leave. Carl's voice stops me.

"If you can't help me," he says, lucidity back for who knows how long, "promise me you'll kill me. I can't go on like this."

I stand stock still at the door. I can't look at him. He's the only friend I have left.

"I promise." I close the door and leave him alone in the dark.

Chapter 15

Instinct's an important thing for a guy in my line of work. My gut tells me to duck, I duck. Never done a goddamn thing for my choice in dates, but it's kept me from getting shot more than a few times.

So when I pull out onto Century, merging with a sea of early evening headlights, and it tells me something's hinky, I listen.

I don't notice the Escalade until I've turned onto Sepulveda, heading north. At first I don't think anything about it. It's the low rent choice in gangbanger transportation. Everybody's got one. The ones who can't afford a Mercedes, that is.

Then I remember thinking that the Escalade I saw the other day was following me.

I've been with Carl most of the afternoon. Rush hour traffic hasn't quite started yet, and traffic is lighter the farther we get from the airport. I slow to a crawl forcing the Escalade to match speed, even though it's in the next lane and two cars back. Horns blare behind me for the sin of me not speeding.

I gun the engine and cut a right into a side street, losing the Escalade if only for a minute. I hang another hard right and watch it pull around the corner after me. If I wasn't sure before that it was following me, I am now.

We continue this dance for a couple of blocks. I gun the engine, take a turn, let the SUV catch up. Gun the engine again.

Three runs of this, and I change the pattern. I turn onto a quiet side street, the only sounds the hum of nearby traffic. I pull in front of a row of pre-war houses and Pottery Barn clones. There's no sign of the car yet, but I can hear it peeling down the street trying not to lose me.

I get out of the car, duck behind a Lexus parked in front of me, and wait. It doesn't take long. The Escalade takes the turn too fast, tires squealing, car shuddering over a speed bump. I figure with that much mass and that much speed, they're not exactly able to stop on a dime.

So, I step out in front of them.

I know what's going to happen next. Know it won't hurt. Doesn't make it any easier to keep my eyes open, make sure I've got a good grip on my gun.

The windshield's got a tint, but not so much that I can't see the look of panic on the two guys in the front. The driver hits the brakes and spins the wheel. The guy in the passenger seat looks like he's screaming. He grabs the wheel, too. Pulls it the other direction. I love teamwork.

The car careens, clipping me with its front fender. I roll off the hood, bounce off the windshield. Feel a bone crack. It doesn't last.

The car rocks to a stop. I pick myself up from the pavement, torn skin filling back in. Limp around the side of the car, feeling bone knit with each step. I watch the guys inside have their minor freak-out.

They're too busy untangling themselves from their seat belts and air bags to notice me at the window until I tap on it with the barrel of the Glock.

I motion them to roll down the tinted window. When it's all the way down I get a really good look at them.

Three Latino kids in the car. Can't be more than seventeen. Two in front, one in back. The kid in the back tries to pull a piece tucked in his waistband.

He stops when I press the barrel to his temple.

"You gonna let me in," I say, "or do I need to make room?"

"Unlock the fuckin' door, man," he says to the driver. "Let him in." The locks pop, and I swing the door open, slide onto the seat next to him. I take the kid's gun, drop it at my feet, stretch out my legs.

"Roomy," I say. "Been thinking about picking one of these up. What's the mileage like?"

They don't say anything.

I press my gun to the back of the driver's skull. "I asked what the mileage is like."

"Pretty crappy," he says, quietly. The smell of piss fills the car.

"Yeah, well. Cadillacs are crap." I sit back, light a cigarette. We sit in silence for a long few minutes.

"So," I say, finally, making them jump. "You want to tell me why you're following me?"

Nothing.

"Or I can just shoot one of you. Pretty sure the other two'll tell me what I want to know. I'm good either way."

"Dude, we're just supposed to watch you," the backseat kid says. "Report back what you do. Where you go. That's it, man." He looks at the floor. "Fuck. Weren't supposed to get caught."

"You working for Neumann?"

The baffled looks on their faces tell me that's a big no.

"The *Bruja*," the driver says. You can hear the capital letter.

The others are staring holes into him. He's probably just committed a major faux pas.

"Go on," I say.

"She wants to know what you're doing, where you're going," he says.

"What the fuck's a *Bruja?*"

"Shut up, man," the backseat kid says. I point the gun at him, and he takes his own advice.

"You were saying?"

"She's a witch. She's THE witch. You don't fuck around with her, man. She tell you to do somethin', you fuckin' go do it."

Interesting. Whoever she is, she's got them all freaked out. Maybe a little more than I do. "She wants to know what I'm doing?"

The driver nods.

"Well, how about I tell her in person?"

"You don't see the *Bruja*," the backseat kid says. "She sees you."

"Today," I tell him, "I think we can change the rules."

———

First guy I ever killed was an Armenian bagman who'd pissed off a jewelry wholesaler downtown. The bagman was holed up in this broken-down brownstone in the Nickel called the Edgewood Arms, with bars on the windows and carpet worn thin from forty years of high-heeled whores, cigarette burns, and bad luck.

Guy had two of his cousins in the room with him. I shot one of them in the thigh. The other one tackled me. I beat him to death with a table leg.

Of course, by then the Armenian was running. I caught up with him in the lobby downstairs just as he was heading out the door. I shot him in the back, and gave the guy at the front desk fifty bucks to forget me.

"You believe in coincidences?" I say as we pull in front of the Edgewood Arms.

The driver looks at me. "The fuck you talkin' about?"

"Probably nothing."

The Edgewood's cleaned up its act. At least as much as any Skid Row flophouse can. Same carpet, same tattered couches. I can't tell if the stain where I shot the Armenian is still there. There's too much competition. The thing that's missing are all the whores and junkies shooting up in corners, but there's something new in the air. Something I don't recognize.

The driver walks up to the front desk, whispers something to the guy manning it. He's looking back and forth between us. Not happy.

The phone rings, and the desk clerk picks it up, says a few things I can't hear, and when he hangs up he's even more shaken.

"She wants to see you," he says.

I don't see any cameras, but I've got a gut feeling the *Bruja* didn't need any to know I'm here.

"Fourth floor," the desk clerk says, pointing at the elevator.

"Don't ya want to take my gun?"

"Nah," he says, laughing like he's sending a Christian to the lions. "Won't do you any good anyway."

A rickety cage, the elevator creaks with the sound of metal too far gone for the task demanded of it. It stops with a brassy lurch a few inches short of my stop, forcing me to step up onto four.

This floor's a little cleaner but not by much. Half the lights are out, and a couple of the rooms are boarded over. There's a girl at the end of the hall, Latina, maybe nineteen or twenty, long black hair, tight jeans and boots. A camouflage T-shirt that says YOU CAN'T SEE ME in white letters. Her arms are crossed in front of her, the universal signal for pissed-off teenager.

"Come on in," she says, voice flat.

I follow her into the room. Done up like an office with a desk, computers and phones, a large map of downtown L.A. on a wall, a bank of filing cabinets. It looks more like a law office than a witch's room.

Like Neumann's place, though, there are symbols on the walls, playing cards stuck in doorjambs and windowframes. Must be a theme.

Besides the girl and me, there's no one else here. I didn't come all the way out here to talk to the *Bruja*'s secretary.

"So, where is she?" I ask.

She stares at me, hands on her hips, says nothing. After a moment of those soft, brown eyes trying to intimidate me, I figure it out.

"You're fuckin' kidding me," I say. "You?" The hard look on that fresh face doesn't fit. The *Bruja*'s a little kid trying to look mean. It makes me grin.

"You have a problem with that?" she says.

Whoever she is, she's got the guys downstairs scared shitless. She's got some weight. And she obviously knows something about me. Best way to play this isn't to intimidate her. That will just make things a bigger pain in the ass.

"No. I'm good," I say. "But seriously. You're not exactly scary."

Something in her eases. She shrugs and sticks her hand out to me to shake. "Gabriela Lupe Cortez. I'm the *Bruja*."

I take her hand. It's warm, and she's got a good grip. She might not look mean, but there's more here than just some little girl playing grown-up.

"You already know my name, I suppose?"

"Joe Sunday. You're a leg-breaker for Simon Patterson. Recently deceased."

"Yeah, he had some bad luck."

"I meant you," she says.

Her stare down might need some work, but her confidence sure as hell doesn't. I outweigh her by a good seventy pounds at least. She's got to know I'm packing. But she takes it all in stride and throws that at me. This little girl's got brass balls.

"You're just full of surprises."

She slips behind her desk, flopping onto the office chair like it's a beanbag.

I take the chair across from her, pull out my cigarettes and lighter. Conspicuously flash the Glock in the shoulder holster. If she notices she doesn't seem to care.

"I'd rather you not smoke," she says. "If you don't mind."

"Uh-huh," I say. "These things'll kill ya." I flick the lighter, but before I can bring it to the end of my Marlboro it goes out. I try it again. Same thing.

"I said, I'd rather you not smoke."

"Fine," I say, putting the cig and the lighter on the desk. If Neumann can give me a light, I suppose she can put it out. Don't see much point in fighting it.

"I suppose you want to know why my men are following you," she says.

"Men? Those kids should still be running around in Underoos. Where the hell did you dig them up, anyway?"

"Locals. I have a reputation around here."

"So I gathered." Somebody whose reputation alone can get these little psychopaths to work together has got to have something to back it up. Impressive. Especially from a kid.

"How old are you, anyway?" I ask. "Sixteen?"

"Fuck you. I'm twenty-five," she says. "And I've got a masters from USC in sociology." She says it like I should be impressed.

"Congratulations. Since you brought it up, why are your 'men' following me?"

"What do you know about magic?"

I can tell she doesn't mean fancy card tricks or guys in tuxedoes pulling doves out of their asses. It's a word I haven't let myself think this whole time. Even with Neumann's tricks, Giavetti's Lazarus routine, I just can't. Sure, I can't explain a goddamn thing, but magic? I'd rather think a virus or a drug or, fuck, something else, even though that all makes even less sense.

But now that she's said the word, now that it's in the open . . . no, I still can't wrap my brain around it. The fuck is it? Might as well have said orgone energy, crystal healing, or angels. It's just another word for Fucked If I Know.

"At the moment," I say, trying to light another cigarette, "All I know is that it's really fucking with my nicotine habit."

Her face breaks into a girl-next-door smile. Her whole face lights up. This is the woman who's got gangbangers shitting their pants when she's not happy? If I were twenty years younger, I might make a play for her on her looks alone.

"It's a lot more common than you might think," she says.

Giavetti and Neumann dance in my brain for a second. "I'm starting to get that, yeah. That how you know my name?"

"It helps."

"All right, you've been following me. Obviously you want something from me. What is it?"

She's playing it off like she planned my coming here. And who knows, maybe she did. "Listen," she says. "There are a lot of people out there like you, you know. Well, not like you exactly. Others. Paranormals, monsters, whatever you want to call them."

"Right," I say. "The vampires are coming for ya, kid. Bleaah." I cross my eyes and waggle my fingers.

She sighs. "They're not like you'd think."

"Wait. Seriously? There are vampires?"

She points to the map on her wall. Multicolored pins jut out of it like a jilted lover's voodoo doll. "There are over a thousand homeless in downtown. You know how many of those are addicts? There are worse things, tougher things to come by than heroin. Vampires are people, like everyone else. And they need help."

I stare at her waiting for the punchline, but it doesn't come. Then it clicks. Young, liberal sociology major. Nobody comes to Skid Row unless they're down and out or trying to save somebody.

I laugh. "You're running a homeless shelter for vampires," I say.

She fixes me with a deep stare. "More than just vampires, but yes. More or less." She leans forward to me, face intense. "You think tweakers are bad off, you should see a vampire gone a week without a fix. They get it where they can. Sharing needles, turning tricks. Most of them are HIV positive, or they've got Hep C. It's like any addiction, only closer to needing oxygen than heroin. And they live a long time, regardless. They need help."

"That's great," I say. "Very noble. The fuck does any of this have to do with me?"

"You specifically? Not much. Other than you're looking for Giavetti's stone."

Aha. "He's already got it," I say.

"No," she says. "He doesn't."

If she was trying to get a reaction out of me, she did a great job. "I'm all ears," I say.

"He was spotted in Hollywood earlier today. He's asking after it. Thinks people know where it might have gone to ground. I want it."

If he doesn't have the stone, then who the hell broke into my house and took it?

"You and everybody else. Sorry, I already got an offer on the table."

"Neumann? Please. I don't know what he's promised you, but I can guess. And I can tell you he can't deliver. And if he could, he wouldn't. He's leading you on."

"Like I hadn't figured that out already. But it's the only offer I got, and I don't see you ponying up to the bar."

"Best thing you can do is get that stone to someone safe. Someone who won't use it. Someone like me."

"Yeah, and why's that?"

Her brow furrows. My skin prickles. I don't know what she's doing but I can guess. Some magic crap. Whatever it is doesn't seem to be working because she frowns like she's just run into a knot she can't untie.

"Nice try," I say. I'm betting she's used to getting her way with less talking.

"Can't blame a girl," she says, trying to pass it off as nothing. "Let me try a different tack," she says. "Magic's a complicated thing. It's energy, everywhere, pools of it all over the place."

"Connecting everything. Yeah, I get it. I've seen *Star Wars*."

"No. It doesn't connect a single thing. It just sits there. You want to use it, you tap into it, like siphoning off gas. But when you do that, it disturbs the pond. Makes ripples. Maybe a little splash. You take a little, but it comes back eventually. People don't make a big splash. We're just pebbles. Maybe at most a bowling ball."

"And Giavetti's stone is a bowling ball," I say. "Big splash. Big fuckin' deal."

"More like a landslide. The well's been getting dangerously close to empty since Giavetti got to town. Two nights ago it almost drained completely. Where were you at the time, Joe? I'm betting you were dead, and Giavetti brought you back to life."

I start to say something, but she cuts me off. "I know he's aging slowly," she says. "How slowly I'm not sure, but he's pretty old. And if he's experimenting with the stone and using more and more of the local well each time, he's planning on doing more than just keeping himself from dying. I think he's trying to do to himself what he did to you but more so. Make himself younger, maybe? I'm really not sure.

"But I do know," she continues, "that if he empties the pool it's going to take a while to refill. Maybe a long while. Days. Weeks, even. There's only so much in an area. Every time he uses it, the magic stops working for everybody else because the stone pulls so much from the pool and splashes so much out."

"I'm still not seeing the point."

"What do you think is keeping you alive, Joe?"

She's got you there, Sunday. I try to light my cigarette again, forgetting for a moment she won't let me. Put the pack away.

"Okay. So somebody uses the stone around here, and I'm fucked. What's it to you?"

"Somebody uses that stone and a lot of people are fucked. You're not the only one running off all that energy."

"So you want the stone to, what, keep it from being used?"

"Exactly."

Interesting. Either she really is a do-gooder, or she's just blowing smoke up my ass like everybody else.

"I still don't hear you offering anything might make me want to find it for you," I say. "That's what you want, right? For me to find it? You haven't said anything that solves my little rotting problem. I figure you already know about that."

She nods. "I do. And yes, I want you to find it. Look, I can't bring you back. From what I know, it can't be done. I can't promise to keep you from falling apart, either. I don't know how to do that."

"So what can you give me?"

"Information. Maybe some answers for you."

"Maybe?"

"My source is . . . fickle."

"Yeah? What source is that?"

"I've got a demon in the bar downstairs. Would you like to meet him?"

Chapter 16

"He calls himself Darius," she says, "though that's not his real name."

"But he's a demon? Like horns and a tail? Shit like that?"

"You're really out of your element here, aren't you?"

"No, I'm fine. Just wanted—" Hell, who am I trying to kid? "Yeah, actually. I don't know what the fuck's going on."

"Fair enough. He's a demon. He says he's an incubus, but I think he's just horny." I have no idea what that means, but it doesn't sound good.

She pulls the elevator door shut with a clatter, and we head down to the lobby.

"Okay, I'm gonna stop you here. What's your piece in all this? Why do you care about the stone?"

"I told you," she says. "There are over a thousand homeless—"

"No. You're some kind of uberwitch running this—whatever the fuck this little empire is you've got. There's more to it. There always is."

Her mouth twists like she's just bit into a lemon. She's not used to explaining herself. She doesn't like it.

"I bought this place about two years ago while I was working on my masters. My thesis was the effects of gentrification on homeless populations. Mostly I just wanted to get out here, help the people I knew wouldn't, couldn't get help. Just wanted to give something back, you know what I mean?"

"Not really," I say. "So, how'd you get into this whole *Bruja* gig? Seems pretty sweet if you can make the gangbangers jump."

"It's more of a pain in the ass than you'd think. I was born this way. My family's been doing this for generations in Mexico. My mom tried to get away from it by moving up here in the seventies, but when I started seeing things that others couldn't, she finally gave in."

"So, this *Bruja* act. It's all real?"

She nods. "It is. I just took who I am and mixed it up with what I wanted to do." She shrugs. "At heart I'm a social worker. It'll get easier as I get older. Nobody wants to take a sorority girl seriously."

"Jesus Christ," I say. "I've seen some crazy shit in the last two days, but I think you might be the craziest."

"Tell me about it. One day I'm picking through applications for jobs with the county, the next day I'm doing this." Looking at her, I don't take her seriously, either. But she's got a disarming smile. There's something about her that tells me I don't want to play poker with her. She might look sweet and innocent, but there's ambition and hunger behind her eyes, too.

The question I'm not asking is, Why is she telling me all this? I'm an outsider. I'm not part of her cause, one of her rescue cases. She says she doesn't let a lot of people see her. So why me?

There's more to this story. Has to be. No one decides to do this kind of dirty work down here unless there's something personal in it.

The elevator stops, and I pull the cage open, four pairs of eyes stare at me.

"He ain't dead," one of her crew says.

"Last one didn't die, either," another answers.

"No, but his hair turned white, and he looked like he'd aged thirty years."

I look over at Gabriela when I hear that. Was Carl here? Did she do that to him? Nothing in her face gives it away.

Gabriela puts a finger to her lips, mouthing, "I'm not here." I decide to play along.

"Man, I'm dyin' to know," the backseat kid says. "What's she look like? She as scary as they say?"

"Yeah. Face like a mule's ass," I say. Gabriela gives me a dirty look.

"Don't go disrespecting the *Bruja*," says the desk clerk. He sounds mean and pissed off. "I'll kill you if you do that again." He turns to her crew. "And you all. You question and you know what happens. You want to end up like that other? He was young when he came in, like you. She'll put you into the ground as nothing but skin and bone." He crosses himself.

Gabriela rolls her eyes, mimes picking up a telephone and dialing a number. The phone on the desk rings. Desk clerk goes back to answer it, his face turning white as Gabriela speaks, her voice an old crone's cracked whisper.

"Let him into the bar. He's not to be harmed. And if you threaten him again, I'll have you skinned." She hangs up her imaginary phone and waves me forward.

We pass the desk clerk shaking at the telephone, as if wondering if his flesh is about to be torn off. I'd pay money to see that.

She leads me to a dark oak door with leather paneling. They're all watching me. None of them noticing her.

The door is the only thing in this sordid room that looks even remotely clean. I don't remember it from when I killed the Armenian. It's placed wrong. If I'm doing the math right, this should open out onto the street.

It doesn't.

There's a jazz bar where Skid Row should be. Be at home in Harlem in the fifties. Smoky red lighting, the bustle of waiters and waitresses, people drinking, laughing, and listening to a live quartet on the stage.

"This shouldn't be here."

"It isn't." She leads me to an empty table near the bar.

"I'm gonna ignore that for the moment. What happened out there? Why couldn't they see you?"

"Oh, come on," she says. "Don't tell me you haven't looked at my chest." She points to her tee shirt where the words YOU CAN'T SEE ME are glowing.

"Didn't think you meant it literally."

"You should see what I can do with bumper stickers. It's best if the normals don't know what I look like. They wouldn't understand."

Normals. Everybody else. People like the gangbangers, the desk clerk. People like Carl. Is that why she's telling me things? Is that why she's showing me her face? Because I'm not one of them? Because I'm not normal?

"What was that they said about making somebody old?"

"*La Eme*," she says. "Mexican Mafia likes to mess with me from time to time. Thinks my men should be running drugs for them. Thinks I should be paying them off. I take threats seriously."

Too bad Simon's dead. He'd have loved her.

I'm not sure I believe her, but nothing tells me she's lying. I file the thought away to chew on later.

"Where are we? And who are all these people?"

"Haven't a clue. In fact, I'm not even sure this is really a place. More a state of mind. Technically, it's not real. Not like *you* see reality, anyway. And the people? Most of them aren't real, either."

A waiter in a sharp tuxedo stops by our table to take our drink orders. Scotch for me. Rum and coke for her.

The band on stage is doing some smoky number, the kind to wind down a crowd before closing. It's good just to listen to it. The customers are more into each other than the music, flirting with each other, laughing at each other's jokes. We spend the few minutes listening to the music before the waiter returns with our drinks.

I take a sip. "Seems pretty real to me."

"Real enough."

"So, where's this demon? He gonna pop out of the stage with horns and a pitchfork?"

"No. That's him over there, tending the bar." She waves at a massive black man with a thin goatee and arms like tree trunks. He's chatting up a smoking hot blonde in a red dress and fuck-me pumps.

"Come on, I'll introduce you."

We make our way through the tables. I can hear the chatter. Most of it's unintelligible—different languages, different accents.

"Darius," Gabriela says, shouldering her way past the blonde, who gives her a dirty look.

"Go on, darlin'," Darius says, deep voice a Barry White rumble. "We'll catch up later." She narrows her eyes at all of us and wanders off in a huff.

"Darius, this is Joe Sunday. Joe, Darius."

"The Dead Man," Darius says, grabbing my hand and shaking it furiously. He's got a grip like an industrial crusher. "I've been watching you, Dead Man. You're all kinds of interesting."

"Glad to meet you, too," I say.

"You should be. Darlin'," he says to Gabriela, "you come to finally give me some of your sweet, sweet honey?"

"You know the rules, Darius."

He rolls his eyes. "Rules are for pussies. How about you, Dead Man? Care for a ride?" He gives me a leer that would make a porn star blush.

"Like you said, I'm a dead man."

"Doesn't mean your equipment don't work." He grabs his crotch and rocks his pelvis at me. "Think about it. I'm always here."

He pulls multicolored bottles from shelves, from under the well, pouring them into a shaker with ice.

"The lady here says you might have some information for me."

"Buy low, sell high." He pours his concoction into a couple of martini glasses, where it swirls like Timothy Leary's brain, full of colors and light. He pushes the drinks toward us. They smell like chocolate.

"The drinks are on the house, but information's expensive. What do you have to trade?"

Gabriela gives Darius a sour look. "It's on my tab. The usual terms."

"Ooooh," he says. "She likes you." He punches my shoulder playfully. "Stud."

He leans in to me and looks me in the eye. "Okay, the usual terms, then. This is how it works, Dead Man. You get three questions, I'll give you three answers. And if you don't like my answers, tough. *Comprendes?*"

"Three questions. How do I know you're telling the truth? That you even know the truth?"

"You don't. But Gabriela here can vouch for me. Of course, there's no telling if you can trust her."

"And this doesn't cost me anything?"

"The lady's picking up the bill on this one."

"Wait," Gabriela says. "I pick up the tab when he agrees to give me the stone."

"Ah," Darius says, leaning back and crossing his arms. "I love a wrinkle. So, what'll it be, Dead Man? Do you give the stone to her, or do you keep it to yourself? Hand it off to the Nazi and see what he does with it? Or hang onto it and stop your rotting?"

"Wait. What did you say?"

"You asshole," Gabriela says.

Darius smiles. Big white teeth. "I always find negotiations more interesting when all the cards are on the table, don't you?"

"The fuck are you not telling me?"

Gabriela rubs her eyes with her palms. "Dammit. Fine. The only reason you're rotting is because you don't have the stone near you. Stay away from it too long and the connection starts to fade. It won't kill you, not really dead, but you'll be little more than a mummy."

Of course. I should have made the connection. "So, if I have the stone I can stop the rotting without having to—" I can't bring myself to say it.

"Eat a whore?" Darius finishes for me, causing a startled look from Gabriela.

"Yeah," I say. "Thanks."

"Anytime, Dead Man."

"Wait, what happened?" Gabriela asks.

"The Dead Man here's got a way with the ladies. Knows the way to a woman's heart." He makes clawing motions in the air. "Grab under the sternum and pull. After all, a heart a day keeps the rotting away."

"I lost control of myself," I say. "Killed a woman and ate her heart."

"But he didn't fuck her first," Darius says. "Because that would be wrong." He puts his hands to his cheeks and makes an O of his mouth, like that *Scream* painting.

"Hey," I say, at Gabriela's horrified look, "at least I'm not eating brains."

"Eh, they're not so bad," Darius says. "Look, you want answers, Dead Man, you best talk to me. My joint, my rules. Now it's time to choose. Do you take the lady up on her offer and maybe find out? Or do you keep her out of the loop and take it all for yourself? And in case you're thinking of

taking the deal and blowing town, I don't take well to dirty welchers."
Again with the teeth. "And you don't want to be known as a dirty welcher,
do you?"

Not by him, no. I don't like the idea of seeing that face in a dark alley.

"If all I need is to keep the stone, then why the fuck should I bring it
to you?" I say. This little girl tried to fuck me over. At least that's behavior
I can understand. I think I actually like her a little better because of it.

"How about this," she says. "If you find the stone and can get it to me,
it's mine. Provided I can find a way to keep you from disintegrating without having to eat hearts. Is that good enough?"

"You said you can't reverse the process."

"I can't, and that's not what I'm offering. If I can keep you from going
all George Romero I get the stone. Keep eating people, and you'll get
caught eventually."

I don't like the loopholes, but it's a better, more honest deal than I've
gotten so far. She knows I want the answers, but I think she knows I'll
walk away if I don't like the deal.

"Okay," I say, finally. "I'll take it."

Darius claps his hands like thunder. "Now, see. That wasn't so bad,
was it? Drink up to seal the deal." He pushes the martini glasses closer
to us.

Gabriela picks hers up, sips it warily. She's not happy about this. I'm
not too thrilled with it either.

"I have to admit," she says, "that's one of your better mixes."

"Thank you, darlin'. I work in vain to please you."

I take a sip of my drink. She's right. It is good. Tastes like spring rain,
oranges ripe off the tree.

"So, I get three questions?"

"Can't you just savor the moment, Dead Man? Gotta go rushin' here
and there."

"The dead travel fast," Gabriela says. "Go on. Answer his questions."

I don't know what price Gabriela's paying for this, but I don't want to
have to do the same. I ask the obvious.

"Where's the stone?"

He laughs. "Oh, my man. You think Gabriela here hasn't asked that one a thousand times? You know what I say to her? I say, 'Darlin', why it's right where you're lookin',' but she doesn't understand. So, how about this? It's closer than you think."

"The fuck kind of answer is that?"

"The one you got."

"All right, this is bullshit." I get up from the bar, head toward the door, customers looking up to watch me stalk out.

"Joe, wait," Gabriela says. "There's a reason he can't be more specific. The stone won't let him."

I stop just before reaching the door. "The hell does that mean?"

"It means that there's a spell that's hiding it. He knows where it is, but he can't say directly. I didn't even know about the stone until I noticed the magic draining and asked him why."

"Great, so I wasted a fucking question."

"I don't think so," she says, taking my arm and pulling me back to the bar. "Just ask your other questions. He won't lie to you, and he's not that cryptic unless he has to be. There are rules he has to follow."

I slide back onto the barstool, Darius smiling a wolf's grin. He claps his hands again, shimmies his head side to side like an Egyptian. A crazed genie in a tuxedo.

"Ask your second question," he says, clearly loving this game.

"What's gonna happen to me if Giavetti pulls the trigger on his plan?"

"Oooh," Darius says. "Good one. Why, son, you'll rot away like old fish in a septic tank. You want details?" I start to tell him no, but he barrels on, anyway.

"Why, your skin's gonna peel off your bones, and it's all gonna go black and splotchy. And you'll leak pus. And then shit's gonna fall off. You thought what you been through was bad? This is gonna be worse. Cause you're gonna lose yourself. Mind's gonna slip away, and you'll feel it slippin', too." He cackles. "And it's gonna hurt. Gonna hurt like it should, your skin sloughing off like boiled chicken skin in a scaldin' pot. And then—"

I cut him off. "That's good," I say. "I got the point." I wonder if this is a con game. As far as I know this guy's just got some fancy tricks up his sleeve. What if he is a demon? The fuck does that even mean? Aren't demons supposed to trick you into losing your soul or something?

My gut's telling me he's being honest. Ultimately, my gut's the only thing I can count on.

Darius puts three fingers into the air like a Boy Scout salute. "Third question," he says. "Make it count."

Fuck. He can't tell me where the stone is. A thousand questions run through my head. Finally I settle on one.

"How do I kill Giavetti? Permanently?"

"Old age."

"You're fuckin' kidding me," I say.

"Son, Giavetti ain't immortal, just very long lived. Stick around another couple hundred years, time'll solve that problem."

"Fuck you," I say. "I asked you a goddamn question, and you give me this bullshit answer."

I'm tired of having my chain yanked. Demon, my ass. I draw my Glock. I don't know why. Maybe because the thought of putting a couple rounds through this jackass's head makes me feel a whole hell of a lot better.

"Whoa," Gabriela says. "What the hell are you doing?"

"Dead Man gotta show me his dick still works," Darius says. "Gotta go wavin' it around for everyone to see."

"Are you gonna give me a straight fucking answer?"

"Or you'll pop a cap in my ass?" He leans toward me. "Go for it, boy."

That does it. I pull the trigger. Behind me Gabriela swears loudly.

The bullet passes through Darius like he's made out of water. Bottles of phantom alcohol behind him explode as they're hit.

Darius looks at the destruction behind him, then back at me. He reaches over and, before I can duck away, he tweaks my nose.

"I like you," he says. "You're cute."

"That's enough," Gabriela says, her voice like iron. "Give him a real answer."

"Oh, fine," he says. "Only thing's gonna kill him is to make sure there's nothing of him left to grow back from. Beyond that, old age is your best bet."

He looks from Gabriela to me and back again. "Happy now?"

Not really, no.

Chapter 17

I'm pacing in Gabriela's office. She's sitting in her chair, bare feet up on her desk, hair pulled back in a ponytail.

"Any idea what he meant by 'It's closer than you think'?" she asks, eyes watching me go back and forth like a caged animals.

"No idea. What about you? 'It's where you've been looking.' Is that what he said?"

"Something like that, yeah."

Darius clammed up after dropping that little bomb on how to kill Giavelti, so we didn't hang around. The gangbangers were gone when we stepped back into the Edgewood, and the guy at the desk was snoring in a chair in the lobby.

"So where have you been looking that's closer than I think?" I ask.

"God, where haven't I looked? I had guys scour the sanitarium in the canyon and break into your house looking for it."

"You what?"

"I deal with vampires and demons. You think a little B&E's going to stop me?"

"When was this?"

"After you went to the club. One of my guys called me and told me where you were. I figured you'd be a while, so I had them toss your house."

"And they didn't find it?"

"No. You had it?"

"Until that night. Somebody must have hit my place before and grabbed it. Unless one of your boys has it in his pocket?"

She frowns, clearly not liking this idea. "I'll check on it, but they know what will happen to them if they cross me."

"Exactly what does happen if they cross you?"

"Depends on my mood. I skinned a guy last week."

"You don't look the type."

"Never piss off a sorority girl. I do what I have to. Any idea who might have known it was there?"

"Giavetti was still in the morgue. Neumann didn't know I had it or he wouldn't have bothered grabbing me."

"Anyone else?"

I shake my head, but Samantha comes to mind. She was at the club with me and could have hit my place while I was at Neumann's. I don't want to mention her until I know what her part is in all this.

"Where else have you looked?" I ask.

"The house it was stolen from."

"One of your guys crack the glass in the front door?"

"That was the dybbuk, but, yeah. You were there, too?"

"Earlier today." I don't know what a dybbuk is. I don't really want to find out.

"Then you were around the airport?" she asks.

"About that," I say, and tell her about Carl. Who he is and how I found him. I don't mention the address he gave me. So far it's the only lead I have, and I'm not giving that one up.

"Jesus," she says. "An eye in his forehead? That's fucked up. I've heard of Neumann pulling some weird shit before, but, damn."

"But he didn't make Carl old."

"You sure?"

"That's what Carl says."

"Any idea who did?"

I don't say anything.

She picks up on my look and returns it just as coolly, no expression on her face. "You think I did it. Because of what I did to the guy from the Mexican Mafia," she says.

"If you did, I'll be really pissed off."

"No," she says. "I didn't do it. I'm certainly capable of it, but it wasn't me."

My bullshit detector still isn't going off. Either it's completely offline, or she's telling the truth. "Any clue who else could have done it?"

She gives a exasperated little grunt. "I can think of twenty people off the top of my head, but only Neumann would have cared enough to try. But you say he showed up after that." She drums her fingers on her desk. "I'm less concerned with who and more concerned with why."

"Carl must have found something out."

"Yeah, but that's not what I mean. Someone could have made him forget and could have kept him in the room, but they didn't need to make him old like that. No, this was because someone was hiding their tracks."

"You've lost me."

"Making a person forget is easy if you do it over time. The house-cleaners in Bel Air probably had their memories chipped away at for a while. It doesn't pull a lot of power out of the well, and nobody's going to notice. But do it fast and for a strong recent memory? That takes a lot of juice."

"Somebody would have caught that?" I say.

"Oh, hell, yeah. Not that they'd necessarily care. A lot of things pull that much power. It's nothing like how much Giavetti's been pulling out with the stone, but it's enough that somebody like me would perk up and wonder what was going on."

"And you haven't noticed anything."

"Nope. Around the time you say it happened, I don't remember so much as a blip."

I get a sinking feeling as I start to pull things together. Images of the desiccated corpses around Giavetti's morgue drawer fill my head.

"They drained Carl to get the power, and that's what aged him," I say.

"Only thing I can think of."

Goddammit. If Carl had stayed the fuck away he wouldn't have gotten himself into this mess. I run through all the ways I could have warned him off better, but I know him. I could have broken his legs, and he would have gone after it anyway.

"I'm still not getting why it would have mattered," I say. "So you notice, so what?"

"It's not easy, but sometimes it's possible to trace that kind of thing back to the person who did it. It sort of taints a person for awhile."

"Like a dye pack in a bag of stolen money."

She nods. "Close enough. But it's a moot point. They didn't pull from the well. They drained it directly out of him." She shakes her head. "That must've hurt."

I can't imagine what that must have been like. Thirty years of your life stripped away just to make you forget something? Roofies would have been kinder.

"So how do we find this person?"

"Hmm? Oh, that's easy. Comparatively speaking. We ask Carl."

"But he doesn't—"

"We ask him after I've gotten him here and fiddled with the memory wipe," she says, cutting me off. "I'll have somebody pick him up. I might be able to get something out of him."

"He can't leave the room."

"I'll take care of your friend. He'll be fine."

I'm not convinced, but Carl needs to get out of there and if she knows something about what's happened to him maybe she can help. And maybe she can get some answers.

I don't want to think about it anymore. "What did Darius mean by the 'usual terms' for answering my questions? How do you pay him?"

"Prostitutes."

"Excuse me?"

"Prostitutes. You know, sex workers. He likes redheads, though he's not that picky. Men, women, as long as he can get his rocks off."

"You hire hookers to feed the demon?"

"I suppose you could look at it that way, but no. He has sex with them. And they're not typical prostitutes."

The phone on her desk rings. "Speaking of which," she picks it up. She listens a bit then says, "Yeah, send her up."

"That one of them?"

"Yeah. You'll see what I mean."

A few minutes later a woman in a tube top and short skirt pokes her head around the door. She's rail thin, copper hair in a teased mess, stark red lipstick glows from her pale face. Sores at the corner of her lips. Looks like she hasn't seen the sun in years. Needle tracks all up and down the insides of her arms.

"Hey," she says.

"Looking for an advance, Patty?"

"Well, yeah. Not really. I just . . . I just thought I could get some before going in to see Darius. He means well, but I gotta have my strength or he, you know, hurts." She brings her knees together as she says it.

"Yeah, no problem. A unit now and a unit after? A-Positive work for you?"

"Oh, could ya? That'd be great. Really great."

Gabriela gets up from her chair, goes to a small fridge, and pulls out a plastic pouch of blood. The Red Cross logo right there on the front. Gabriela tosses the bag to the vampire, and she catches it with a little panic on her face.

If she's paying them off in blood, she's got to have a steady supply. And if she can get blood, can she get other things? Hearts maybe?

"Go ahead and use the bathroom by the elevator," Gabriela says.

Patty nods and disappears back down the hall. She's not paying attention, anymore. Gabriela's right. Tweakers have it easy.

She takes a deep breath. Lets it out slowly.

"You do what you have to, right?" I say.

"Yeah," she says. "You got a problem with it?"

"All things considered, I don't think I'm in a position to judge."

"Oh, right. Forgot who I was talking to there for a second. It's just that I want to make things better. I keep an autoclave in the bathroom. Fresh needles. Tell them to use that, but they all have their own works, their own little rituals. They never listen. Patty's so loaded with shit, if she was a normal she'd have died years ago. No telling how long she'll last."

"You can't save everybody."

"Don't fucking tell me what I can and can't do." She lightens up. "Words of wisdom from the zombie hitman? I'll keep it in mind. Darius'll be happy. He likes Patty."

"Then you've done your good deed for the day and fed the homeless." I look at my watch. I'm not hungry, but who knows how long the heart I had last night is going to keep me going. "Speaking of which, I should probably leave."

"I'll have somebody take you to your car," she says, reconsiders. "Unless you're going to eat them?"

"No," I say. "I think I'm good." If Darius isn't just yanking my chain, I'm going to have to figure something out and soon. I don't like the idea of having to hide more corpses.

"Remember our deal, Joe."

"I will if you will."

She walks me to the elevator. Waves at me as I'm going down. Like it's the end of our first date or something.

I pick up my car near the airport and head home. I'm about fifteen minutes up the freeway when my phone rings.

Carl. I fumble it open. "Yeah?"

If I thought he was freaked out before, he's completely lost it now.

"Man, you gotta get over here," he says, voice ragged. "There's somebody wants to talk to you. Like, right the fuck now. I think—" And the line goes dead.

Fuck. I drop the phone, gun the engine. Pray I don't get there too late.

Chapter 18

I hear the yelling through the elevator doors. Hotel guests are losing their minds, poking panicked heads out of rooms to watch the nightmare down the hall.

The wall opposite Carl's door is sprayed bright red, lines of it looping up to the ceiling. The door ripped off its hinges. From the inside.

I flash my fake badge at the nearest security guard, and he almost pisses himself in relief. Finally, somebody with authority showing up to deal with this mess.

Carl's on the floor in shock. A stump where his left arm used to be. A hotel doctor's tying off a tourniquet.

I don't see the arm anywhere. All the furniture has been tossed over, lights on the floor throwing crazy shadows along the walls. The doctor is screaming something.

I realize it's me he's yelling at. I pull myself together. "Put pressure here," he says, yanking me down to the floor. He shoves my hand over a thick gauze pad that quickly soaks with blood.

The pillowcase is barely on Carl's forehead. I pull it tighter.

Long gashes along his cheeks. Looks like something big with claws raked him across the face. He's so far gone he doesn't even recognize me.

"The hell happened?" I ask the doctor.

"The fuck should I know," he says, looking Carl over for more wounds. "I get a call from the front desk saying there's a panther in here, and somebody's screaming. I get up here and see this."

There's a commotion in the hall. Security guards letting somebody through.

Gabriela pokes her head through the doorway. She's leading a gurney with one of her gangbangers. Both dressed in jeans and blue shirts which have "Hi, My Name Is:" stickers with the word "Paramedic" scrawled on them. The stickers glow a light blue and no one seems to notice that they're not the real deal.

She catches sight of me and gives me a what-the-fuck look but doesn't break character.

The doctor is barking orders at her. "We've got him from here," she tells the doc in a voice pitched low. There's a weird harmonic to it just under my hearing.

"You've got him from here," he says, eyes unfocused.

She passes a hand over Carl's body and the convulsions ease, the blood stops. The doctor backs away as they wheel Carl out the door.

I'm worried Carl's going to burst into flame as they cross the threshold, but he doesn't even flicker.

Gabriela looks over her shoulder and mouths "I'll call you," before she disappears down the hall with Carl's ravaged body.

I give it a second, start to follow her out. My fake badge isn't going to stand up to the scrutiny of real cops the way Gabriela's name tags would.

I'm at the door when I spot something in the corner. A blood-spattered piece of hotel stationery stuck to the shade of an overturned lamp. In large letters it reads:

WHERE'S THE STONE, JOE? —G-

I pick it up before anyone notices and leave.

That cocksucker. Giavetti thinks I have the stone. Instead of coming at me directly, he's trying to fucking intimidate me by hitting Carl. God-dammit.

I don't give in to guilt. Bad for business. Bad for a lot of things. I take a deep breath. I know it does nothing, but it still feels good to put air in my lungs.

Fucking Giavetti.

It isn't enough I'm in this shit because of him, now he does this. Wants to send me a message, piss me off? He's sure as shit done a thorough job.

I'm cleaning blood off my hands in the lobby bathroom when Gabriela calls.

"That was a neat trick in there," I say.

"Thanks. The Force has power over weak minds. It was lucky I headed out just after you left my place. I don't know if he'd be alive if I'd gotten there any later."

"How's he doing?"

"Not good," she says. "I mean, you saw him. But he's not dead yet, and that gives me something to work with. You want to tell me what you were doing there?"

"He called me just as the shit hit the fan." I tell her about Giavetti's note.

"Dude, you are not a good man to be friends with."

I was thinking pretty much the same thing. "Is he awake?"

"Thankfully no, but he's not what you'd call resting peacefully. Look, I have to go. I've got a Honda minivan that everybody thinks is an ambulance and it takes concentration to keep it up. I'll call you when I know more."

"Thanks for doing this," I say.

"This is the kind of thing I live for," she says. "Like I said, I'm a social worker at heart. I'll call you." She hangs up.

I stand there a minute looking at the phone. She's right. If it hadn't been for her Carl would be dead.

If she can keep him alive, maybe she can get something useful out of him. Maybe I can get the stone.

And Giavetti's head on a stick.

The ceiling of the Marriott's parking garage is covered in insulation foam that swallows up sound. I light up a Marlboro, the scratch of the spark disappearing in the echoless underground garage.

Not too many cars, so it's easy to spot them. Not too many places to hide. Something tells me they want to be seen.

"Archie," I say.

He leans against my car, Jughead on all fours at his feet, the midget's tailored black suit scuffing on the cement.

"Mr. Sunday. I'm surprised to see you here."

"Funny, I was just about to say the same to you."

"Quite the show upstairs," he says. "I understand that the police are looking for some sort of wild animal. A panther, I believe, though I over-heard one distressed young woman mention a polar bear. Funny how rumors spread, isn't it?"

"Yeah, funny things. So why are you here, Arch? Checking up on the reporter?"

"That's it exactly," he says. "I understand from Doctor Neumann that you were here earlier. He saw you briefly. I was sent over to see if you had, ah, jarred anything loose."

"Nope. I got nothin', Arch. Now why don't you let me get into my car, and I'll let you get along with your evening."

Archie makes no move to get out of my way. Settles against my hood a little more, in fact. Crosses his arms. Jughead apes his movements from the floor.

"I'm curious," he says. "How did you know to come back to the hotel now? Of all times? In fact, I'm wondering how you knew to come here in the first place. It took Doctor Neumann hours to get a fix on this place, and yet you just happened by. Why is that?"

"I have my sources."

"No doubt," he says. "Would one of those be that young woman pass-ing herself off as a paramedic who carted the reporter away? It's my job to notice things."

Jughead is getting increasingly agitated as Archie gets calmer. It's weird how much the midget looks like a twisted version of Archie.

"Is it? If you'd been doing your job a little better in the first place," I say, looking Archie squarely in the eye, "Neumann wouldn't be replacing your sorry ass with me, now would he?"

Archie gazes impassively at me. Jughead, though, that little fucker's snarling like a trapped wolverine. He moves on me, but Archie gives the leash a quick jerk, snapping the midget back.

"Wouldn't want to let that leash slip, now would you?" I say. "Can't have all those chained-up urges getting loose."

"You don't understand a thing," Archie says. "You're a hammer, nothing more. A badly made, poorly used tool. Doctor Neumann is using you, and you're too stupid to get it. At the end of the day, you don't matter. When he's done with you, he's just going to leave you to rust in the rain."

"Wow. That was almost poetic. I'm hurt. Really."

"Just go away," he says. "Slip quietly into some hole, why don't you? It'll be easier."

I take an inhumanly long draw on my cigarette, put it out on my hand. The skin crackles back, the edges glowing, then fades away as if nothing has happened.

"Easier than what, Arch? The fuck you think you can do to me?"

He leans in toward me. "I'll cut off your head and burn the rest. I'll stick it in a box with enough maggots to chew your eyeballs out and keep you in pieces. And when I want a laugh, I'll open the box and piss in your eyeholes."

"Good. But it still doesn't rhyme. I got a better idea."

I give a swift kick to Jughead's skull, punting him across the floor. With a loud squawk, he spins under a Hummer.

Archie throws a haymaker. I duck under it easily, give a quick punch to the kidneys. Bring my knee up into his stomach, shove him down. Air blows out of him with a loud gasp, his eyes bug out like a fish's.

Before he can get his wind back, I bring both hands down like a hammer onto the back of his neck, bounce his head off the concrete floor. I hear his nose crunch, and I know it's over.

Jughead comes toward me. I have my Glock casually pointed at the back of Archie's head.

"Don't," I say. "I'm not sure you'll survive if I kill him. You want to find out?"

Jughead snarls but keeps his distance. I back into my car seat, gun leveled at Archie as he stands up. His eyes are swelling black, dark blood drips from his busted nose.

"Go home Arch. Get some ice on your face. Leave me the fuck alone."

Chapter 19

It's funny how some things can crystallize your thoughts.

With Carl out of commission I've got no one I can trust. Just as well. It's my mess. I'm the only who can get me out.

The first thing I need to deal with is Giavetti.

No. It's not.

I already know what he's doing. He's trying to tell me that he can get to me at any time. That much is obvious. Trying to freak me out. Go after friends, family. If I had a cat I probably would have found it nailed to my front door. It's an old strategy. I've done it myself.

This kind of thing comes from a position of weakness, trying to make it look like strength. Give me this thing or I'll do this to you. Yeah, and if you could do it to me, you would have already.

So, why doesn't he?

For starters, it's not like he can hurt me. Torture's pointless. Shooting me, more so. If he sticks me in a block of cement, I can't do much talking under eight feet of concrete.

So he goes after my friends. Only I don't have any left. He doesn't have the stone and doesn't know where it is. So, no, he's not the number one priority. I'll kill him later. Once I figure out how.

What about Neumann? Some old fart who can put eyeballs on people. He's not a problem. But Archie is. If he didn't hate me before, he sure as hell does now. I probably should have killed him in the garage.

I'm still on the fence with Gabriela. She's giving me a hand, helping Carl, but she still wants the stone, and she tried to screw me over for it with Darius.

And then there's Samantha.

She's just as much an enigma as when I met her at the club. She knows Giavetti. Had a falling out with him. But she hasn't mentioned the stone. Hasn't tried to convince me to give it to her or to keep it from someone else. Not once.

What the fuck is that all about?

I had meant to track her down after I was done in Bel Air, but then Carl and Gabriela and whatever the fuck Giavetti did in that hotel room happened.

My gut tells me she's not going anywhere. Not until she's seen me. She's got some stake in this and something she wants from me, or she wouldn't have tracked me down at the club, wouldn't have talked to me about Giavetti. So she can wait.

Which leaves me the address I got from Carl.

I don't know if Neumann could only see through the eye or if he could hear through Carl, too. If he can that could be a problem. He could be there now, and god knows what he's finding.

I check the address online. It's east of downtown, next to that cement ditch we call a river. A little more digging, and I realize that it's a junkyard.

I look at the clock. They won't be open. That's fine. Every self-respecting thug has bolt cutters.

———

Most of the time the L.A. River is empty, a long slab of concrete where bums try to sleep while kids with too much drug money race their pimped-out Hondas. Occasionally, when we have rain that's more than a drizzle, we get a lesson in the fact that all that cement's there for a reason.

Our river doesn't flow, it just floods. Every year, some moron gets swept away while helicopters try to pull him out, and the news guys stand by and film it all for our amusement.

I pull up about a block from the yard. The nearby train tracks are quiet. A couple of railcars on side tracks, some semis parked nearby. Anything natural was paved over a long time ago.

Mackay's Salvage. High chain link and razor wire. Cars piled high like Hot Wheels in a windstorm, tumbled together in a maze of scrap metal hallways. A compactor and crane. A trailer for offices in the back.

I don't see much in the way of security, but there's got to be something.

I take a good whiff. Car exhaust, motor oil, and gasoline. Seat leather, vinyl too long in the sun. Something else. There's at least one—no, two people here. One of them really likes garlic, the other's an Old Spice kind of guy.

I wonder what that tastes like.

And a dog. One dog? More? I can't tell.

It takes me almost two minutes to cut through the padlock. These bolt cutters are great on fingers, not so much on industrial steel. I have to stop twice and duck behind an oil drum when the security guards and their lone Doberman pass by. The dog offers me a casual sniff, but beyond that, they don't seem to know I'm here.

I slide the gate open enough to let me through and close it behind me. The place is a fucking maze. Dead end at a mountain of Buicks, just as the guards make another sweep. This time the dog's less forgiving.

Had a dog growing up. I'd hate to have to shoot this one. I check to make sure I've got a round in the chamber, just in case.

I push my way farther in the shadows and wait for the guards to let the dog loose, but they just tell it to shut up. They pass out of earshot, the barking and yelling fading in the distance.

Head to the back, get lost a few times, double back, finally find the offices to one side of the crane. The space they're in is a staging area for feeding cars into the compactor. A rusted-out Cadillac hangs over it from the crane like a dead man on the gallows.

Lock's an expensive Schlage embedded in a cheap wood-paneled door. I could pick it, but why bother? The door pops open under my shoulder.

Pretty boring layout inside. Filing cabinets, couple desks, chairs. A wall calendar showing Miss Tech-Tool September, silicone tits and all.

I riffle through the filing cabinets looking for what, I don't know. They're full of invoices and time sheets.

Then I see it. Sitting at the top of a license to operate, right under "Mackay's Salvage." The parent company: "Imperial Enterprises." And under the words "Sole Proprietor," S. Giavetti.

I stare at it, trying to make sense of it.

I'd almost forgotten about Imperial, the company that owned the house that the stone was stolen from. And Giavetti owned it?

I'm having trouble making sense of it. If he owned the house, if he got the guy in there with the stone, why did he need to hire guys from Simon to steal it? And something else. Other questions, but catching them is like trying to grab at moths. I can't seem to think straight.

Why can't I think? "Fuck me," I say.

"Yeah, gonna do more than that."

I turn to see the guards and their dog right outside the door. Thought I'd closed it better than that. Got so wound up I stopped paying attention to my nose. Still not used to it.

But now that I am, they remind me of beef stew and pumpkin pie. That can't be good.

"You need to walk away now," I say. My voice is thick in my ears. Something's wrong. I realize what as I catch a glimpse of my hands in the guard's flashlight. They've started to sink in on themselves, and splotches of rot are starting to bloom along my knuckles.

"Tough talk," one of the guards says. Older guy. Overweight. Too many donuts and not enough exercise. His partner's just a scrawny kid with acne scars. Doubt he could bench press a third his own weight with those arms.

The dog, though, all lean muscle and hungry teeth. And disciplined. Staring at me, not growling, not barking. Waiting for the command to go get himself an early breakfast.

"Really," I say. "You want to run." I lurch at them, try to barrel my way past. I don't want to kill them. They haven't done anything.

But then the fat guard lets the leash slip, launching the Doberman at me like a shot out of a gun, and I lose control.

The dog takes my arm. Teeth sink into my sleeve. My leather jacket keeps it from breaking skin, but the bone underneath crunches.

They're expecting me to drop, scream, do something that will let them come in and beat on me with batons. They don't expect me to bum rush them. The Doberman scrabbles for better purchase on my arm. Jaws lock down tighter.

I push my way out the door. Swing the dog at their surprised faces. Patches of hair are falling out of my head, skin still attached.

The kid gets the dog's ass upside his skull, knocking him to the ground. I pick him up with my other hand, launch him toward a pile of rusted-out junk. Twisted metal rains down onto him, pinning his legs. I dislodge the Doberman, throw it after him.

The fat guard draws his gun and gets a shot off that punches through my chest, out my back. Quick step in, jab in his kidneys, sweep the gun out of his hand.

I give him one last chance. One chance to run, get out of here and save himself. I lean down at him to tell him that he can go, but he has to go now.

All that comes out is a groan.

He swings his flashlight up, freezes when he sees how far gone I am. A chunk of flesh falls from my jaw and plops onto his face. That's the last straw. He starts to scream.

I grab the light, beat him until he shuts up. Beat him until his face is nothing but bloody pulp, busted teeth.

Then I start in on his sternum, the Maglite cracking through bone.

There's a whimper nearby. I look up to see the kid staring at me and shitting himself.

"Don't worry, buddy," I try to say, "you're next."

But all that comes out of my mouth is a torrent of thick, black blood.

When I come to my senses, most of the Doberman's back end has gone down the fat guard's gullet. Loops of canine intestines hang between his teeth. Chest is a ragged hole. Most of his lower jaw is missing.

Doesn't look like it stopped him from making short work of his buddy.

Pinned under a half-dismantled Studebaker, the kid didn't stand a chance. His neck is chewed through and most of his chest is gone.

He's still pinned, but he's already moving. Sweeps his arms back and forth, like he's playing a game of blind man's bluff.

I wipe thick blood off my watch. Damn. All this carnage in half an hour.

Just like last time I'm back to normal, covered in gore and chunks of rotting skin. I pull myself up from the ground. The fat guard casts a quick glance over his shoulder at me and goes back to work on the dog's corpse.

I come up behind him, grab his head, snap his neck. He drops like a sack of bones. I take his partner out too, separate the dog's head from its neck for good measure. Last thing this city needs are zombie dogs.

Getting rid of the bodies takes a little while, mostly to lever the kid out from under the Studebaker.

I toss them into the top loader of one of the junkyard's car compactors. Turn them into paste with the push of a button.

I don't feel the same kind of disgust I did with the whore. Because she was a woman? Because I hunted her down? Because I can rationalize this one better? They did set a dog on me, after all.

Maybe I'm just getting a taste for it.

This is getting insane. I can't be killing people and making zombies every night. Eventually, somebody's going to notice. What if one of them gets loose?

I hose myself off and cover my front seat with a tarp. Maybe I should hose my car out, too.

No answers just more questions. What the fuck is Imperial Enterprises? Giavetti's company. He's been around god knows how long, he's got to have put together a decent bankroll.

It doesn't make sense. The guy who owned the stone lived in a house owned by Imperial Enterprises. Why would Giavetti get him in there and then steal it from him? Unless that was part of the plan. If the stone's in the house then it's vulnerable. Giavetti would have had access to all the security codes. He could have arranged for anybody to just waltz in and get it. Even three thugs without a brain cell between them.

Giavetti's got twists and turns that I can't begin to figure out. That's part of my problem. I don't know him, not really.

I need to talk to someone who does.

Chapter 20

Samantha's building is a 1920s Mediterranean-style hotel converted into condos overlooking the bluffs in Santa Monica. It's surrounded by buildings half its age with half its character.

The sun is just a hazy glow on the eastern horizon, peeking over the rooftops like it's not sure it wants to get up. Less than three blocks from the beach, her building is shrouded in the early morning fog coming off the Pacific. I step through a small gate into the central courtyard, water dripping off the wrought iron bars. The fog will burn off in an hour, but right now it might as well be London.

Finding her wasn't tough. After taking a shower to get all the slime off me, all I had to do was hit Google.

Something about her that I haven't been able to shake since I met her in the club. She's not my type, but then I'm not sure you can call strippers and washed-up porn starlets a type. My dates aren't known for their conversational skills.

Maybe that's what it is. She's different. I can't pin her down. She's something between normal and the weird-ass rabbit hole I've fallen down.

Maybe it's just because she hasn't hit me up for Giavetti's stone yet.

There's a doorman who looks more like a bouncer standing just inside the foyer. I was hoping for a surprise entrance. Bang on her door. Catch her tired with her guard down.

"Who are you here to see, sir?" he says, like it's noon and strangers wander into the building all the time. I can smell gun oil on him, barely make out the telltale bulge under his armpit.

"Samantha Morgan."

"And you are?"

"Joe Sunday."

"Go right on up, sir," he says, gesturing toward the elevator. "She's expecting you. The elevator will take you to the penthouse."

I look at my watch. "She say when she was expecting me?"

"Couldn't say, sir. She called down about fifteen minutes ago to let me know you were coming."

So much for the surprise entrance.

The elevator lets me off right inside a foyer decked out in teak and mahogany, and the minute I see her I know I'm out of my league.

Samantha's waiting for me in a rattan chair next to a potted palm. A white sundress, strappy sandals. A thin, gold chain around one ankle. Hair pulled back in a ponytail.

"You were hoping to catch me in my pajamas, weren't you?" she says as I step out of the elevator.

"Something like that."

"Joke's on you. I don't wear any." She glances over my shoulder at a clock on the wall. "I'm off my game," she says, sipping a cup of tea. "I expected you here ten minutes ago."

"I like to keep people guessing," I say.

"Of that I have no doubt." She stands and steps toward me. Too close. Her scent is overpowering. I could get drunk off it. For a second I'm afraid I'm about to zombie out. But this is different. It's not hunger, not like that, but it's definitely desire.

She looks up into my eyes, studies my face. "I was starting to think maybe you didn't like me," she says.

"No chance of that," I say before I can stop myself.

Her face breaks into a smile. "Good."

I pull myself together. "But that's not why I'm here."

She sighs. "Of course not. Come on. I've more comfortable rooms than this one."

She leads me through a wide connecting hall into a living room of dark hardwood floors, wrought iron, stained glass. The place is something between a Moorish castle and an art museum. Asian and African masks litter the walls.

And playing cards, like at Neumann's and Gabriela's. But done up like art, not stuffed haphazardly into doorjambs. Collages, mosaics. Antique cards mounted on the wall behind glass like miniature portraits.

She leads me into a living room filled with plush chairs and sofas. French doors open onto the penthouse deck. Fog so close I could touch it, the ocean nothing but a hint of sea air.

"What's with the cards?" I say, following her to a sofa. "I didn't know it was such the in thing."

She glances at them. "Sort of a security system."

Something I've been thinking about after seeing Gabriela's shirt keeping her invisible. It's as if magic is more about the metaphor than the reality. A camouflage shirt to hide yourself, miming a telephone to call a real one. All of the cards I've seen are face cards. "Eyes and ears?" I say, thinking I've caught on.

"No," she says, "but I get what you're going for. It's more like," she pauses, searching for a word. "Static. All the cards have personalities. Tarot cards are best, but playing cards are pretty much the same thing. Some people would see us sitting in a crowded room. Much more difficult for those sorts of people to see past it all."

"Huh. And I just thought you all had a gambling fetish."

"Sorry. I'm more a fishnets and leather kind of gal. And much as I'd hoped, I don't suppose that's what you came to talk to me about."

Fishnets, leather, and her is a powerful image, and it throws me for a moment. "No," I say, finally. "I need to talk to you about Giavetti."

"I figured as much. He did something rude, didn't he? I swear that man is like a five-year-old with a hand grenade."

"He ripped a guy's arm off in a hotel at the airport."

"Is that all?"

"He was a friend of mine."

She stops, her face softening.

"I'm sorry," she says. "I—I know that sounded callous. It's sort of a defense mechanism, and sometimes I forget things. How to be. . . . I'm very sorry."

"Not your fault," I say. I don't know what it was she was about to say. I let it slide.

"Can I do anything to help?"

I can think of a good dozen things, none of which will get me closer to Giavetti. "You ever hear of Imperial Enterprises?"

She cocks an eyebrow. "You've been busy."

"You know it?"

"Sandro has investments. A good dozen companies set up to handle his finances. Most of them are legitimate. Some aren't."

"So it's his company?"

"One of them, yes. I'm sure he has others that I don't know about. I think he uses this one to handle property on the Pacific Rim, but I'm not sure."

"How do you know about it?"

She gives me a Don't-Be-Stupid look. "I keep tabs on him. I thought that much was obvious. We used to be sort of an item. Back in the day."

"Still got a thing for him?"

"Please. Sandro is *sooo* yesterday. I broke it off with him a long time ago."

"How long?" The way she moves, the way she's acting. She's sure of herself, that much is certain, but there's something else under that. Something not quite right. I've got an idea, but I want to hear her say it.

"I'm so rude," she says, changing the subject. "Can I get you a drink or something? You must think I'm a horrible host." She hurries through to the kitchen. I get up and follow her.

"I'm good, thanks."

"Well, I need a refill." She fills her cup from a silver teapot on the stove.

I try a different tack. "How'd it end?"

She winces. "Badly. Sandro's been looking for immortality, some kind of fountain of youth since before I met him. He's never been entirely successful. At least not on himself."

"His coming back from the dead trick?"

She nods. "That's right. You saw him in the morgue, didn't you? You saw the other bodies? How they were desiccated? I don't know exactly how he does it, but how long it takes him to come back depends on what's around him. One time he was dead for over three years."

"You know why he looks so old?"

She laughs. "It's because he is. He's still aging, just very slowly. But he's been around a very long time."

"You said 'not on himself.'" I get an image of more people who turned out like Julio. I wonder if any of them turned out like me. "He's always experimented on others first?"

"Of course. He's not stupid. That's what finally made me leave him."

"What happened?"

She gives me a look like I'm dense, and when I figure it out, I realize I am.

"How old are you?" I ask.

"How old do I look?"

"About twenty-three."

"I'm hurt," she says with a little pout. "When he murdered me I was nineteen."

Chapter 21

"What the hell does that mean?"

She gives me a sly smile. I follow her back into the living room. "I need something stronger than tea," she says. She pours brandy into a glass, curls up on the couch. The way she drapes herself, curling up against its back, she might as well be a cat. I never really had a good idea what "lithe" meant. Now I know.

I flop into the chair opposite her. The silence stretches out. I'm the one who finally breaks it.

"He brought you back," I say. "Like me."

She shakes her head. "Not quite." She sets down her drink, reaches over the coffee table between us to take my hand. Compared to my room temperature mitt, her hands are burning up.

"You're still warm," I say.

"I'm still alive." She turns my hand in hers, her fingers delicate against my wrist. "Does it hurt? Not having a heartbeat? Not breathing?"

"No," I say. "I don't feel a thing."

She lets my hand fall, and a look of something passes her face. Is it envy?

"I got the immortality Sandro wanted for himself," she says. "He made a deal with something in East Africa," she says. "I was never very clear on what. And if he'd trusted it, we probably wouldn't be having this conversation. But he decided to try it out on me first."

"And he had to kill you to do it?"

She nods. "It was . . . unpleasant. And when he tried to do it again on himself, the thing he'd bargained with told him it was a one-shot deal." She laughs. "He slit his throat like he'd slit mine. Took him three days to come back from that one. He'd wasted his chance at living forever on me. Last I heard, the thing he'd bargained with wasn't returning his calls."

"So you can't die?"

"Not permanently. A day, maybe two at most. It's like waking up from a bad dream, and I go on about my day."

"Must be nice." I wouldn't mind the whole living forever thing if I wasn't rotting once a day.

"It's been useful a time or two," she says.

"You know, you still haven't told me how old you are."

"Nobody's ever told you it's rude to ask a lady that question?" When I don't answer the glib pretense falls away. She closes her eyes, almost as if she's ashamed.

"I'll be four hundred eight in January," she says. "At least, I think it's January. We weren't quite as big on calendars back then."

That's what it is. All of her charm and poise is well practiced, but it's like she's going off a script. It's slightly unnatural.

After four hundred years, she's forgotten how to be normal.

She gets up, moves to the open French doors facing away from me. "I knew you were going to ask that," she says. "But I still wish you hadn't."

I come up behind her. She leans back into me, all warm and soft. I put my arms around her, not sure what I'm doing but knowing that it feels right.

"I'm sorry," I say and mean it. And I'm even sorrier for my next question. "What's your angle in this? Neumann I get. Giavetti I get. But what about you?"

"Sandro is about seven hundred years old," she says. She lets me chew on that one for a moment. I knew he was old, but seven hundred years is a number that doesn't fit in my head. Four hundred is bad enough. It's good information to know. Fucking frightening, but still. I nod, and she continues.

"I met him when I was eight," she says. "He protected me, raised me. When I was old enough to not be a child to him anymore, he was my lover. You don't know this yet, but living this long is a special kind of lonely. I've lost count of the times I've been married. How many lovers I've had. There's only one man I've known almost my entire life. I can't turn my back on him. Everyone I've known has died or will die. Everyone but me and Sandro. And now you."

"I'm not sure I'm up for four hundred years," I say.

"Do you think I am? It's not like I've had much of a choice. I'm going to live forever whether I want to or not."

Suddenly it makes sense. "Giavetti came to you for help." Of course. Who could he trust with his search to become immortal except the only person he knew who wouldn't need it.

"Yes," she says. "I hadn't seen him in a long time. He was so old. He knew the stone was here and had some ideas how to get it. But he needed cash. So I helped him out. He came to Los Angeles because he heard someone here had it. I leant him some money. All of his assets are tied up in companies like Imperial Enterprises. He's got no liquidity. When I heard things fell apart the other night, I needed to know what happened to him. I wasn't entirely sure he'd be back. He'd always managed to before, but I'd never seen him so old before. I just wasn't sure." She shudders. "It scared me. I don't love him, haven't in a long time. But I can't just let him die."

"And that's where I came in. You're playing me to find him."

"No," she says suddenly. Her eyes earnest. "Yes. I mean—I was. Before I talked to you. Before I knew what had happened. You're going to live forever, and I know how lonely that is. And I thought. . . ." Her words hang in the air.

"You know I need the stone, right?"

"What do you mean?"

"I'm tied to it or something. I'm not real clear on how. But if I'm away from it too long I start to . . . fall apart."

"Oh god. I had no idea. You have it, right? I mean, you're okay?"

I shake my head. "I did. But somebody stole it."

"But you look fine."

"It's temporary. I have to—well, the less said about that the better."

"That's why you're looking for Sandro? You think he has the stone?"

"I did. But after last night I don't know." I pull out the blood-spattered note I took from Carl's room and hand it to her. It's a quick read.

"So it's still out there," she says, eyes thoughtful.

"He's been asking around for it."

"If he finds it, you'll never see it again."

"Probably not."

She touches my face, caresses my cheek. "I'm sorry. I don't know what I can do. I just met you and now—"

"And now?"

She answers by kissing me. She's warm, burning hot, and her lips taste like cherries.

I could fall into her. She's got eyes like an angel or a devil, but I can't tell which. I'm not sure I care. I imagine waking up to her wrapped around me, sheets tangling us together.

Then I remember I don't sleep anymore.

I push her away. "I don't trust you," I say. And I don't, but I want to.

"You will."

"We can't," I say. "You said it yourself, I'm not like you. I'm dead."

She gives me the wickedest grin I've ever seen. Probably give Darius a run for his money. "Young man," she says. "Don't tell me what I can and can't do." She slides up against me, her heat warming me through.

I step back. "No. Who the fuck's got the stone? You? How much of what you're telling me is bullshit? I can't tell if you're yanking my chain. I can't tell a goddamn thing with you."

"Trust," Samantha says. "You come in here, grill me about my life. Accuse me of, god I don't know what. I open up and tell you everything. You have no fucking idea how hard that is." Her eyes go from ocean blue to pale ice.

"I'm sorry."

"So am I," she says. "Get out."

———

I stalk past the security guard downstairs. He's smart enough to give me a wide berth.

I should go back up there. Beat what I need to know out of her. It wouldn't do a bit of good. What's the worst I could do to her that she hasn't seen in four hundred years? Or lived through?

But that's just a rationalization. Truth is, I don't want to. I'm really not sure what I want.

I drive north along the coast to clear my head, turn my thoughts toward Giavetti.

So he made a deal with a devil, and he got screwed. I wonder if Darius knows anything about that, but push the thought away. It'd be like asking some random guy if he knows your cousin who happens to live in the same state.

My phone rings. I answer it before seeing that it's Danny's cell. "The fuck do you want?"

"Look, I know we got off on the wrong foot the other night." He sounds wrong. Tentative. That's not the Danny I know.

"Quit groveling. It sounds weird coming from you. What do you want?"

"Dude, I'm just trying to make amends." His voice is definitely shaky. Whatever the deal is, he's freaked.

"Which means you want something. Get to it or I hang up."

"I don't want anything. I just— Look, that old crazy guy? The one that killed Simon? He's not dead."

Yeah, no shit. "You saw him?"

"Fuck, did I see him. Comes looking for you last night out behind the club. I tell him I'm not your secretary, and he pulls a fucking dog out of thin fucking air. Goddamn thing tore Bruno's face right off. He's sitting in Cedars with tubes in his head."

"A dog?"

"A mastiff or something. But bigger."

Bigger than a mastiff. Big enough to maybe tear Carl's arm out of its socket?

"Okay, calm the hell down," I say.

"Fuck you. I am calm. What the hell is going on? You know some-thing, don't you?"

"It's complicated," I say. "He say anything else? Where he'd be?"

"Said he'd be at the club tonight. Dude, he's looking for you. If you don't show, he's gonna send that fucking dog after me. You gotta be there."

"I'll think about it."

"No, seriously—" I hang up on him.

Giavetti at the club tonight. He thinks I've got the stone. I don't know why he thinks Danny and I are friends.

Much as it would be fun to let Giavetti's dog eat Danny, I'm going to be there. It's too good an opportunity.

I need to get him off my back. Killing him might buy me some time, but who knows how long? All that would do is piss him off, and there's no guarantee that I'll have the stone before he comes back at me. And if he's got a giant dog with him, now, that might be too hard to pull off anyway.

An idea slowly builds in my head. It's probably bad, and I don't really want to do it, but the more I think about it, the more I think it might work.

If I can get it to work.

I punch in Frank's number. It rings a couple times before he picks up.

"The fuck do you want?" he says with that same tone of contempt I had with Danny. His voice is more haggard than before. A little slurred. Dammit.

"Are you drunk?" I say. "It's not even eight a.m."

"Fuck you." I can tell he's about to hang up the phone.

"Hang on," I say. "Sorry. None of my business. Look, I got a bead on Giavetti," I say. "If you want him."

That gets his attention. "Yeah? Where's he?"

"You know Simon's old club? In Hollywood?"

"Place near, what, Cherokee? Yeah. I know it. He there now?"

"Tonight. Don't know when, but they don't open until ten. He's looking for me and threatened to kill somebody if I don't show up."

Frank laughs. "He doesn't know you very well, does he? So the fuck do you want me to do about it?"

"Thought you'd like to know where he'd be. Was kind of thinking that if you could bring some of your fat cop buddies with you, you could get him locked up for a few days until you figure out what to do with him. No chance of him just walking out of County. Not with L.A.'s finest watching him."

Silence. He's thinking about it. "You gonna be there?"

"Yeah," I say. "I'll get him inside. Stall him. You do whatever cop shit you need to do and get him in a cell. Or into an abandoned warehouse. Or wherever. You'll think of something creative to do to him, I'm sure."

"I don't know," he says.

"He killed your brother," I say. "Look, shoot him for all I care. Throw him in your trunk and wait for him to come back to life. I'm just trying to help you out. Jesus, this isn't rocket science. Just lock him up."

"And get him out of your hair?" he says. "That's what you want, right? He's looking for you, isn't he?"

No sense in lying to him about that. "Yeah," I say. "Get him to leave me the fuck alone for a few days. Alive. I don't need to be worrying that he'll wander out of the morgue again."

"Fine. I'll be there tonight. See what I can do."

"Good. Best chance you'll have at him, buddy."

He's already hung up.

Chapter 22

The Edgewood Arms is just as ugly in the daytime. I wonder what Gabriela sees in the place.

I park across the street, passing a couple of old Mexicans sharing a can of Colt 45. Classy.

The old Latino guy at the desk glares at me through yellowing eyes. "She's in the bar," he says.

"Thanks."

He laughs. "Don't thank me, *pendejo*." He covers his ears with his hands. "Enjoy the noise."

I don't know what he's talking about until I open the door to the bar and run into the screaming.

This isn't just regular screaming. This is cats-being-fucked-in-the-ass-with-a-two-by-four screaming.

The bar has been replaced with what looks like a World War I-era field hospital. Sunlight streams through windows that aren't there. A cool breeze blows down from lazy ceiling fans. Young men, bandaged, bleeding, or missing limbs lie on beds behind mosquito netting screaming for their mothers.

"The fuck is all this?" I say over the noise, spying Darius and Gabriela at the end of a long row of beds. Darius is dressed like an old-time doctor in a white lab coat and a headband reflector. He waggles his eyebrows at me like Groucho Marx as I come near.

Gabriela has a look of disgusted exasperation. She points at Darius. "He won't shut them up."

"I just thought your friend might feel solidarity among these honorable wounded," he hollers over the sound.

It's then that I realize they're both standing over Carl's bed. He's only vaguely conscious.

"I doubt all this noise is helping him."

Darius waves it off. "Oh, hell, he can't hear 'em. I'm just doing this for verisimilitude."

"See?" Gabriela says. Clearly, she doesn't have any actual control over Darius. If she's at all worried about that, she doesn't show it. I try a different tack.

"Would you mind dropping the volume a bit?" I say. "Please?"

"For you, sahib, anything," he says and bows to me with his hands together. The room falls silent except for Carl's low moans.

"You couldn't have done that sooner?" she asks Darius. "Thank you," she says to me, not waiting for the demon's answer.

"How is he?"

"He'll live," Gabriela says. "But he's a mess. Darius has him stabilized."

"I live to serve," Darius says.

The stump of Carl's arm is neatly bandaged. He's been strapped down, but even so he's thrashing about on the bed.

"Can he talk?"

"Not so far," Gabriela says. "Somebody really did a number on him."

"You can help him, though. Right?"

"That's what we're trying to find out," she says. "We've managed to block the link between Neumann and that eye on his forehead, but that's all. I'm having a problem."

"The thing that kept him in the room or made him forget?"

"Neither, actually. I think I know how to get rid of those. Problem is that although I've altered Neumann's work, I don't know how to reverse it. As long as it's there it's in the way. I can't do anything about the other spells until I take care of what he did."

"Not as easy as pulling a plug?"

"Sure, if I knew where the plug is. Sometimes it's obvious, but, and I hate to say this, he's good. Better than I thought, actually."

"So you need Neumann?"

"I think so, yeah," she says. "Think if you ask him nice he'll take it off?"

I don't answer her.

"Yeah," she says. "Didn't think so."

———

Where the Edgewood Arms is just as much a shithole in the daylight, Neumann's mansion is radically different. It looks deceptively normal.

Archie's waxing the Bentley when I get to the gate. He sees me and comes over, sleeves rolled up to his elbows, tattooed arms that would put the Yakuza to shame. They're all patterns and words, none in English as far as I can see.

"Mr. Sunday," he says behind steel bars, gritting his teeth. "We weren't expecting you."

"Nice shiner you got there, Arch," I say pointing at the purple and black ring around his eye. "It looks really painful."

"Is there something I can do for you?"

"Yeah, I need to have a conversation with the old man. Neumann in?"

He stares at me, like he's trying to read my soul. Good for me. Pretty sure I don't have one anymore.

"I'll see if he's available." The tone in his voice said "fuck you." He turns and heads toward the house.

"Hey," I say. "Where's the midget?" I thought those two were inseparable.

"Eating squirrels," he says over his shoulder, disappearing into the house. I don't think he's joking with me.

There aren't any security cameras that I can see, but I don't doubt that Neumann has eyes everywhere—certainly if Carl's anything to go by.

They don't keep me waiting long. The gate slides open on a well-oiled track, the front door opening as I approach, then closes behind me. Archie, waiting inside the foyer.

"More magic?" Funny how the word just slides out now. I must have gotten all the way through to Acceptance.

He shows me a remote. "Sometimes modern conveniences are easier. He's in the library. Follow me."

Neumann's sitting at the same table where I first met him, a thick book in front of him. "Joe," he says, all smiles. "How are you? Come to give me good news, I hope? You found the stone?"

"A lead," I say.

"Excellent, excellent. Then follow up on it. Why are you here?"

"I need something from you first."

"Money." I can almost smell the acid in his tone.

"No. I need you to undo whatever the hell it is you did to the reporter."

He leans back in his chair, honest surprise in his face. "Ah, yes. The reporter. I saw you in his room the other night and Archie told me of your, ah, encounter. I've also noticed that I can't see through the eye I gave him. But then you already know that, don't you?"

I nod. "He's got information, but that thing you put on his forehead's keeping him from giving it up."

"Really," he says. "That's fascinating. Now, I don't suppose you came to this understanding all by yourself?" He stands, starts to pace.

I know that look. That's the look of someone figuring out something he doesn't like. I can feel Archie behind me. I wonder, when it comes down to it, who I'll need to kill first.

"I'm outsourcing."

"How industrious of you. Who is he?"

"A guy I know. Not your problem. You gonna pull it, or do I let the lead go and lose your stone?"

His eyes are weighing me. "I see. You know, Joe, I don't think I care for the direction our partnership has gone. I think it's time we dissolved it. I think it would be better for both of us."

Archie takes that as his cue and makes his move. I've been watching him edge his way behind me since I walked in here, and I'm ready for him.

He's faster than I give him credit for. Barely get a chance to twitch before he has me in a half nelson, my gun arm useless. He brings his other hand around with a pistol in it. Close enough, I'll have a hole in my head I wasn't planning on.

It's not a bad move. If I were him, I'd probably try the same thing. Too bad for him it won't work.

I drop to one knee, tear my shoulder out of joint. The momentum pulls him down with me. He grunts, surprised, his shot tears a furrow across my skull.

I aim a backward kick at his knee. A loud pop and a wheezing inhale tells me I hit.

I leverage him over my shoulder, flip him into a desk. He crashes and rolls. By the time he's up my shoulder's back in joint, and I've got my Glock on him. He's sweating, knee swollen.

"I don't want to have to kill you, Doc. I just want you to take your goddamn magic shit off the reporter."

"What did Giavetti offer you, huh? It's him, isn't it? Is that it? Or is it a woman? It's that bitch, isn't it? She's been trouble since I met her."

"Last chance."

"Or what, you kill me? Torture me?" He laughs.

"Not you, no," I say and shoot Archie in his good leg. He screams and goes down. "Boy's still got two good arms and a head. I could make this last."

"You don't know what you're fucking with, young man."

Seems he's right. I'm paying too much attention to Neumann and Archie. A mistake I figure out a second too late.

The midget comes at my head like a cannonball. Claws rake across my neck, cutting to bone, teeth latch onto my shoulder, shredding the tendons. My arm goes useless and the gun drops from my hand.

He moves onto my neck, trying to chew my head off. Making pretty good progress, too. I can't reach him, so I throw myself, back first, into a bookshelf a couple of times. Hard enough to stun him. He goes so slack I can grab his legs and pull.

Fucker's got jaws like a pit bull. He rips off my shoulder, and even then he's still working at a chunk of meat he's torn out of me.

"You're gonna have to do more than toss dwarfs at me, Doc."

"Good idea," Archie says, lunging up at me from the floor, but I'm ready for him. I swing Jughead up and over, slamming him into Archie's skull like a baseball bat. There's a crack like shattering wood, and he drops to the floor.

I beat him a couple more times with the midget, but he's not staying down, pulling himself up on torn and shredded legs. He makes a grab for Jughead, jerking him out of my grasp, throwing me off balance. He tosses the midget aside, broken and limp, like a rag doll.

Archie's legs are shredded muscle and tendon, but he's standing on them anyway. Before I can get my balance back, he's got me in a better hold. Dislocating my shoulder isn't going to work this time.

"Well, that was exciting," Neumann says. He looks over at Jughead's broken body. A discarded toy tossed on the junk heap. "Pity. I'll have to make a new one."

He turns his attention back to me. "I'm so sorry we couldn't work this out, Mr. Sunday, but you've given me hope, if that's any consolation."

"Makes me warm all over."

"I thought it might. Now that I know what's getting in the way of that reporter's unfortunate memory loss, I just need to bring him here." He raises my Glock toward my head.

"You know that's not gonna kill me."

"I don't need to kill you. I just need to put you out long enough to drop you down a hole."

Archie's taken the hint and shoved my head far enough away from him to not get hit. Perfect. The change in angle is just what I need.

Pull my knees up, lean forward. The sudden shift in weight pulls Archie down on top of me just as Neumann pulls the trigger.

Not sure if the bullet hits Archie or the other way around. Either way, his head explodes in a shower of red and white. His body convulses as Neumann shrieks like a girl. I shrug Archie's dead weight off of me, roll to the side and onto my feet before Neumann can readjust his aim. The Doc gets a wild shot off. Puts a hole into an expensive looking book.

I sweep the gun out of his hand before he can bring it around at me. I'm in the middle of a good right hook that should dislocate the old man's jaw when his fingers twitch.

I get thrown back like I've been hit with a semi.

I fly across the room, too stunned to register what's happening. Stop inches from the wall. Hang in midair. This is not good.

Like a bug pinned to a board I can move my arms and legs, but the rest of me is stuck to . . . well, to nothing.

Neumann steps just out of range of my flailing kicks. Scowls, rubs his hand where I knocked the gun from it. "Archie told me you were going to be a pain in the ass." He looks over at the corpse.

"Should have listened to him," I say. "He might still have his head. And his midget." I see my gun sitting on the floor under a desk. Might as well be in another state.

"I think I'm done talking to you," Neumann says.

"Oh come on, Doc, I was just getting star—" And I'm flying through the air again.

This time it's a bookshelf that stops me. Hard. At least three ribs crack. The shelves crunch from the impact. Books fall to the floor.

I try to grab the shelf. This is just the start. I get a good grip on an edge, but the force of Neumann's pull is too strong. Back in the air. Face-plant into a wall.

My nose crunches. Rinse, repeat. Bones are healing fast, but they're barely back in one piece before I hit something new.

Neumann doesn't seem to be getting tired of this game. Cackling like a five-year-old who's just learned he can set ants on fire. How long can my body hold out before it's used up?

I'm moving so fast everything's a blur. Keep spitting out new teeth. Lost count of how many times my nose has been broken.

Another bookshelf. Instead of holding on, I reach out and snag the biggest, fattest book I can get my hands on: a leather-bound, twenty-pound atlas.

"You're a bug, Sunday," Neumann screams. "And I'm going to keep squashing you until there's nothing left." He hurls me away from the wall.

And as I go by I throw the book at him.

Not sure it's going to work. He can probably stop it in midair like he can stop me. From the look of surprise right before it slams into his head, I think it caught him off guard.

Momentum disappears. I hit the floor, skid into an overturned desk I've hit three times before.

I limp over to Neumann as my legs heal. He's pushing the book off of him, eyes unfocused, blood running from his nose and mouth.

"That must have hurt a lot," I say. I pick up a broken table leg from the floor, heft it in both hands. "This'll hurt more."

I step on his chest and run the ragged end of the table leg through his throat and into the floor where it sticks.

Neumann convulses, uselessly pulls at the leg. Tries to scream. Pretty sure I've taken out his vocal cords. Blood gushes around the wood jammed through his throat.

I grab a nearby letter opener, get onto my knees, look him in the eyes. "You're gonna suffocate soon, if you don't bleed out first. And I want you alive for this."

I jam the letter opener down just below his sternum, reach in with my hand, and start to yank. He gurgles, flails.

"The hell of it is, Doc," I say, tearing his sternum away from his ribs, "I'm not even hungry."

Chapter 23

I need new clothes. The midget made a mess of me when he chewed through my neck. Should have killed him when I met him. Neumann's blood hasn't helped.

I'm strangely okay with eating the Doc. Not the best way to kill a person who's pissed you off, but it's pretty damn satisfying.

I blacked out again while I was ripping out Neumann's heart. Lost control. Took out a lot more than I had planned. By the time I come back to my senses, there's a lot of blood, a lot of bone. Not much meat.

My phone rings. It's slick with blood and hard to get open.

"Yeah."

"I don't know how you convinced him to do it," Gabriela says, "but the spell's off. Carl's still got the eye, though. I don't think I can get rid of it. What'd you do to convince Neumann?"

"Ate him."

Silence.

"Okay, then," she says and hangs up the phone.

No one's going to walk in on me, so I take my time cleaning up my mess. Neumann never got up like the others. Figure it's because some time during my feeding frenzy I tore his head off.

When you have a lot of uninterrupted time you can really take the care you need to dispose of a body. I cut them up with an electric carving knife I find in the kitchen, bury their bits in the backyard.

I find some of Archie's clothes in a bedroom. They're not a perfect fit, but they're not covered in guts, so that's a plus. I shower and change.

The house is enormous, and it takes a couple more hours to toss the place. Most of this crap is useless to me, or I don't know what it is so it might as well be. Eventually I find some papers with the Imperial Enterprises letterhead.

It's paperwork acknowledging Neumann's bid at an auction and then later pulling out of the bid. It takes a few minutes to parse out the legalese to figure out it's for the book he wrote that he was trying to get back. The one he figured out was a forgery that ultimately went to Giavetti.

So Imperial Enterprises was running the auction? So Giavetti already had the book. So why auction it off in the first place?

Maybe he didn't know what he had until later?

I'm getting fucking tired of more questions than I've got answers for.

———

I check in with Gabriela a few times throughout the day. See if Carl's said anything yet. So far, he's still out. I tell her I'll be by later and if anything changes to call me. I don't need to play nursemaid to him. Darius and Gabriela have that covered.

I've got nowhere to be for a few hours. I head home. Spend a lot of time pacing, cleaning the house, finally putting things back in order from when Giavetti ransacked it. But there's only so much cleaning a guy can do.

It's funny how you don't notice how much time gets taken up by things you have to do until you don't have to do them anymore. Eating, sleeping. Going to the bathroom.

Seriously, I haven't gone to the can since this happened to me. Where does it all go? I'm not gaining weight, and god knows I've eaten enough. Neumann was a hell of a lot more than a cheeseburger and a side of fries.

I keep checking myself in the mirror for signs of rot. Keep thinking it's there then decide it's not. I'm getting stupidly OCD about it and force myself to stop.

I don't know if I'm going to have an episode tonight after eating Neumann. Hopefully that will tide me over for another day.

I try to sleep. Not because I'm tired, but because then I could close my eyes and pop them open, and it'd be eight hours later.

Instead I get three hundred cable channels of the same stupid bullshit it's always been. This is what eternity looks like?

By the time I find myself watching an episode of *The View* in Spanish I know it's time to go.

I head out to the club. They don't open for another hour, but I want to get there before Giavetti does. The idea of seeing him tonight, especially after hearing about that monster dog he's got, has me a little spun. So far, nothing's torn any limbs off of me. I assume they'll grow back, but I don't really know.

Hopefully with Frank there Giavetti will have better things to worry about than siccing his dog on me.

The club is still gearing up for the evening. I go in through the back entrance.

The bouncers seem to know I'm coming. They wave me through and give me distance. I get looks that tell me they probably saw last night's fight.

Without the dim lighting the place looks like a Goth warehouse. The walls flat black, the windows painted over. A DJ is setting up on the stage where last time girls in latex were getting whipped while tied to a crucifix.

One of the bouncers I know, big guy who goes by the name Steroid Harry, is over giving a pep talk to the rest of the crew. They're shaken, that's for damn sure. If they didn't see Giavetti pull out his dog, they heard about it. Heard about Bruno.

I catch Harry's eye. He heads over when he's done psyching up his talent.

"Danny tell you what happened last night?" he says.

"Big dog. Bruno in the hospital. Guy wants to see me."

"That's the gist of it, yeah."

"Danny around?"

"Haven't seen him. Cocksucker better be here. These guys are freaked the fuck out. Half of 'em didn't even come in tonight."

I don't blame them. I don't really want to be here myself. "Why are you even open?"

"Danny. Goes on this rant about the bottom line. How nobody's gonna get him to close. Dude, I think he's lost it. I swear, he better show up."

"He'll be here," I say, knowing he won't.

I can't imagine the last few days have been kind to the little cock-sucker. Every mob in town sniffing at his heels wanting to pick up where Simon left off. Nobody's come to me yet, which doesn't surprise me. They have to know Julio's dead, and it's in their best interest to leave me alone. By their thinking, if I get into it they'll take me out, sure, but some of their people will wind up dead. Give it a week. Then I'll start getting phone calls.

With all that and Giavetti, the smart money's on Danny skipping town.

I plant myself at the bar, toss a few drinks back. Wait for the lights to dim and the crowds to show up.

The club fills up before midnight. It's a very different crowd tonight. Strobe lights, glow sticks. Whistles and pacifiers. Everybody's chugging bottled water.

Fuck I feel old.

Another hour goes by and no Danny. The light in his office is still out, and I don't see him. Or smell him. But even through the scents of sweat and drugs filling the club like fog, I do catch a whiff of something familiar.

"Evenin' Joe," says a voice at my elbow. I don't turn, just nurse my drink and try not to snap Giavetti's neck where people can see. And right now, every bouncer in this place is looking at us.

"Giavetti."

"Been looking for you, son," he says, sliding onto the stool next to me.

"So I hear. Doing stupid pet tricks, too, from the sound of it."

He waves the bartender over, who goes white at the sight of him. She remembers last night just fine. He ignores her look, orders a gin and tonic. She backs away slowly to fill it with shaking hands.

"You use what you've got. Sometimes that's not enough."

"Saw some of your work up close the other night. You know, I'm in the phone book. Could've just popped by any time."

He shakes his head. "Like you wouldn't have seen me coming. No, this way I've really got your attention, right? Besides, if your buddy in the hotel room had talked, he'd still be around."

"Think maybe he didn't know anything?" I say.

"Yeah. Eventually. Took me a while to figure that one out. Got the job done, though, right?"

I get up from my stool, hand toward my gun, catch myself just as I realize what he's doing.

He laughs. "You're easy, you know that? All I have to do is say B-5, and you pop up and yell 'Bingo.' Come on. You're not going to kill me with all these people around. And anyway, I'd just do the morgue drawer two-step again."

"Was thinking maybe I'd just dump your ass in a cement mixer this time."

"Like nobody's done that before. Sit the fuck down. We have things to discuss."

I slide back onto my stool, force myself to calm down.

"Way I see it, there are two people who could have the stone," Giavetti says. He sips at his drink. "You or your cop buddy, and he's too stupid to know what it is."

I think about that for a second. Could Frank have it? I ditch the idea almost as fast as it forms. No. I can't buy that. Giavetti's right. Frank's nothing but mindless rage and confusion now. I can't see him knowing how important the stone is. If Frank had it, he'd have done something with it by now.

"Stone won't help you without Neumann's book," I say. "You still have that?"

He stares at me a beat long enough to know that I've hit a nerve. "All right, so you've been digging. Which means you know the Kraut's looking for it, too."

"Not anymore, he's not. I killed him today."

The music fills in the silence between us. I can almost smell the gears burning in his head. How much do I know? Do I have it? Can I do anything with it?

"Well good for you. My offer's still solid, you know. Get the stone to me, I'll bring you back."

I make a show of considering it. Sip my scotch. Watch the floor show a bit.

Where the fuck is Frank? There's only so much stalling I can do.

"You know I've got it," I say. I show him my hand. Not a blemish on it. "Not on me, no, but you know what happens if I'm away from it too long, don't you?" I study his eyes and see the surprise there. "Yeah, I figured that one out already. So, you know what? You gotta do better."

"I don't haggle."

"Fine. I've already got another buyer set up. You don't want it, I'll just go there." I polish off my drink, stand up.

"Hang on." He waves me back to my seat, orders me another scotch. "Son, you're probably the only man in this shithole town with a pair on him. You want to haggle, we haggle. What's this 'other buyer' giving you?"

"We both know you can't bring me back to life, so stop yanking my chain. But if you can make it so I don't rot away, the stone's yours."

"All right," he says. "I can do that."

"And I know you'll try to screw me over. Which is why you get it once you fix me up."

"Kids these days. No respect for their elders. Son, if I want to screw you over, I can think of a dozen ways just off the top of my head. I've had a long time doing this. I'm—"

"About seven hundred years old. Yeah, I know."

Giavetti's looking at me the same way he did when he had me locked away. Not sure what to make of me. Not sure what to do with me.

"Well," he says, all traces of his Chicago accent gone. "So you know more about me than I thought. Congratulations." His voice is thick and Italian. The hard as nails, Chicago mobster act fades away to a smooth, cultured tone. The gravel gone from his voice. "Not many people figure that one out."

"I'm special. Like Jerry's Kids. You know, I saw the security tapes from the morgue. Did you know one of the interns fucked you while you were out? Seriously, they have some messed up people working there."

"You done, kid? Or you got more to get out of your system?" The Chicago is creeping back into his voice. I wonder if he can ever really let go of it. How many personas has he had to hang onto himself? Does he even really know who he is anymore?

I make a show of thinking about that. "Yeah," I say. "I'm done."

"Fine," he says. "So I fix you up, I get the stone."

"Mmmm. No."

"The fuck you mean, no?" he says.

"Changed my mind." Where the fuck is Frank?

"This is horseshit. The fuck do you want, huh? What, do I need to get on my knees and blow you right here?"

"There's a thought."

"You're pissing me off, kid," he says. "Last time I'm gonna ask. The fuck do you want?"

"Cash. A huge fucking wad of cash. I want a fistful of thousands and a start in a new town. Between you, Neumann, that fucking cop, and the bullshit going on in this joint, this has been the worst goddamn week I've ever had. I'd just as soon pull up stakes and head someplace else."

"How much are you talking?"

"A quarter million. That, and keep me from going all George Romero, and you get the stone."

"You're out of your fucking mind."

"That's the deal."

Giavetti taps his fingers on the bar, thinking hard. "Gonna take me time to get that much cash. Can't do it tonight. Tomorrow night, though. I'll bring the money. You bring the stone. That work for you?"

I catch a whiff of Aqua Velva behind us and relax. Time to let this one close. "Tomorrow's fine," I say.

"Tomorrow's fine for what?" Frank steps in behind us. Need to work on that.

"Why, if it isn't Barney Fife," Giavetti says. "Evening officer."

"Funny meeting you two here," Frank says. He's dressed as casually as he can be, in a Hawaiian shirt and slacks. But his body language screams police. He could have taken a cue from some of the vice cops that come in here.

"What, with me being dead and all?" Giavetti says.

"Pull up a chair, detective," I say. "Join the chat."

Giavetti gives me a what-the-fuck-are-you-doing look, but I ignore him. What I'm wondering is where Frank's backup is, and how come they didn't swarm in and grab Giavetti. Frank could have gotten him on some bullshit charge. God knows he's done it to me enough times.

Frank's got the manila envelope in his hand. Same one he showed me in the diner.

"Didn't think you'd remember me," Frank says.

"I never forget an asshole. Especially one that kills me. You don't seem surprised."

Frank opens the envelope and pulls reports, photos, everything he showed me. Plops them in front of Giavetti.

Giavetti leafs through the papers, chuckling at some of the pictures, scowling at others.

"Wow. I used to be one handsome motherfucker, huh? You've really done your homework, son. I'm impressed. You want to tell me what this is about?"

Frank pulls one last picture out of the envelope and places it in front of him. Giavetti stares at it for a few moments, looks at Frank.

"Oh. Him. Yeah, I remember him. So, it's revenge, then? Well, you killed me already. Congratulations." He sips at his drink.

This is not going the way I expected. I should have known this would happen. Of course, Frank isn't going to act like a cop. He's been hunting this sonofabitch down for too long. He's got some sort of plan, and I'm not a part of it. Jesus, I'm an idiot.

"I'm not here to kill you," Frank says. He hands Giavetti a folded piece of paper.

Giavetti takes it, tentative. He opens it and reads what's inside. No reaction. I'm watching this whole thing like it's playing out in a movie.

"What are you doing, Frank?"

"Shut up, Joe. You got yours." What the fuck does that mean?

Giavetti looks up at Frank. "I'll think about it."

"You do that. But don't wait too long. Time's running out."

Frank stands up. Doesn't even look at me. Turns to go. I grab his arm, and he shakes it off.

"Don't," he says, seething, and stalks off into the crowd. I start to go after him, but Giavetti stops me.

"That was an amazing coincidence, wasn't it? Him showing up here like that? Why it's almost like he knew I was going to be here."

"Don't look at me," I say lamely. There's no pulling out, now that it's all gone to shit.

"Of course," he says. "Whatever could I have been thinking? So you bring the stone here tomorrow night, and I show up with a quarter mil in cash. I solve your problem. You solve mine. Everybody's happy. You good?"

No, I'm not good. I'm fucked. I watch Frank fade into the crowd. I don't know what the hell just happened, but it's bad whatever it is.

"I'm good," I say, because I can't think of anything else.

Chapter 24

Giavetti stands. I start to follow him. He puts his finger up to stop me. "No," he says. "I'll see you tomorrow. Don't follow me. My little doggie won't like it."

I let him go, though I know I should follow him. Put a bullet in his brain outside the club. Buy me some time. But that giant dog that stuck Bruno in the hospital would be a problem.

Doubt I can kill him and get away before he sics it on me. Or before the cops show and throw me in the can. Doubt Frank would try to bail me out now. Spending a night in a cell would be a really bad idea.

I punch Frank's number in my phone. Cocksucker's not answering. I need to get answers. I can probably track him down, but I have to leave now.

Outside there's no sign of Frank or Giavetti. The line to the club stretches halfway down the block.

My phone rings. I flip it open hoping he's calling me back. The hinges stick a little. There's still blood in it.

"Where are you?" I ask.

"At the Edgewood," Gabriela says. "Where else would I be?"

Shit. "What is it?" I'm still looking up and down the street, hoping to spot him crossing the street or driving a car. Nothing.

"Thought you might want to know your friend's better. And not screaming. An improvement overall, I'd say, though Darius has his own opinion on the matter. Are you all right?"

"Not really," I say. "So, he's up? Has he said anything useful?"

"Not yet. And 'up' is a relative term. He goes in and out of consciousness, but mostly he's just resting. It's been a long night."

"Okay," I say. Maybe the night won't be a total wash. "I'll be there in a little bit. Twenty minutes or so."

"I'll be here. Uh—"

"What?"

"When you said you ate Neumann, that wasn't a joke, was it?"

"No," I say.

"Okay. Just checking. Fucker deserved it. I'll see you in a bit."

———

Gabriela's in her office putting pins in the oversized map on her wall. Her long black hair is pulled into a ponytail, and she's back to wearing her camouflage shirt with YOU CAN'T SEE ME printed on the front. She looks exhausted.

"How's the patient doing?" I ask.

"Better, all things considered," Gabriela says. "I moved him out of Darius' place to a room down the hall."

"Can I talk to him?"

"When he wakes up. I gave him a buzzer to let me know when he's up to talking."

"But—"

"He needs rest," she says. "So, what was that on the phone? What happened?"

"I saw Giavetti tonight," I say. "He wants the stone, thinks I have it."

She frowns. "We had an agreement," she says, her tone wary.

"Hang on. It's not like I have it. And it's not like you can help me, either. Right?"

She looks at the floor. "I've been trying. But I haven't gotten very far."

"Figured. Thanks for being honest with me. At least somebody is. Never intended to give it to him, even if I did have it. Just wanted him off my ass. It didn't go as planned."

I tell her about my idea to get Giavetti locked away and Frank's fucking it up.

"What do you think Frank's up to?" she asks.

"Haven't been able to figure it out." Been racking my brains going over it since I left the club. I can't think of anything Frank would want from Giavetti besides revenge for his brother. And what would Giavetti want from Frank? The only thing he's looking for is the stone.

And then I really feel like an idiot.

"What is it?" she asks.

"What did Darius say to us before," I say. "The stone's where I least expect it?"

"Yeah," she says. "And he told me it's right where I'm looking."

"You were following Frank, too, weren't you?"

It hits her. "Son of a bitch."

It makes sense now. Between the time I left him and the time I got back from seeing Neumann, Frank has had more than enough time to run through my place, pry open my safe, and walk off with the stone.

"Then let's go get it," Gabriela says. She starts toward the door when a loud buzzing sounds.

"Carl?" I ask.

She nods. "Hang on." She knocks on a door couple of rooms down the hall and goes in. A moment later she comes out.

"He's awake. More or less. You might not have much time before he passes out again."

My mind's buzzing. I'm itching to go grab the rock. But this is important, too. I make a choice and follow her into the room.

Carl looks better, but he's still a ragged mess. The lines on his face are deep. The stump of his arm heavily bandaged. Looks like he's gone three rounds with Tyson, a pit bull, and one of my ex-girlfriends. He's barely awake. Eyes half-lidded and unfocused. Even the one on his forehead.

"Hey," he says, recognition dawning on his face. "Hey, man. You got me out of that hotel room." His voice is thick. Slurred around the edges. Probably pumped full of morphine.

"Yeah. How are you feeling?"

"A little . . ." His voice trails off, then he focuses on me. "I'm okay. Yeah."

"You remembering any of that stuff you couldn't before?"

He nods. "Couple things."

"Okay." I'm talking slowly, voice low. Keep him soothed. "What happened?"

"I didn't do much. Just looked into that place where your boss died.

It's owned by a company called Imperial Enterprises. They do a lot of import-export. Own a lot of property."

"Like that junkyard you gave me the address for?"

"Yeah. That one was weird. Everything else made sense, you know? Office buildings, a hotel in Hawaii. But a junkyard? It just jumped out at me, you know? Stuck in my mind."

"Imperial's owned by an Italian guy," I say. "Giavetti."

He frowns. "Where'd you hear that? That's the name, yeah, but not some guy. Woman. I called her up and met her at the hotel to ask her some questions. Just on a whim I dropped your name. I don't know why. Thought there might be more there than you were letting on. Told her you were a friend of mine. She knows you."

My stomach does backflips, and it takes Gabriela's hand on my shoulder for me to notice I've balled my hands into fists.

The name on the Imperial Enterprises paperwork I found at the junkyard was S. Giavetti. I assumed it stood for Sandro.

Never occurred to me it might be *Samantha*.

"I'm really tired," Carl says.

"Go back to sleep," Gabriela says. She adjusts a dial on the IV, and he starts to drift off.

"Yeah," I say. "Get some rest. I'll check on you later."

Gabriela ushers me out of the room. I wait until we're back in her office before I start swearing.

"That fucking bitch. I fucking fell for it. The whole fucking thing."

"What are you talking about?" Gabriela says. "What bitch?"

The one thing I've kept from her is Samantha. It seemed the right thing to do at the time. But now I don't know why. I'm such a fucking idiot.

I spill everything to Gabriela. From beginning to end. How I met Samantha, how she led me on about Giavetti.

The more I talk about it the more it all falls into place. Who knows how long she knew about the stone. How long she's had Neumann's book. Years, maybe. Had to be, to have set all this up.

Giavetti didn't have the stone or the book that Imperial had because he isn't Imperial.

Samantha used Imperial to set the stone's owner up at a nice house with lots of security. When Giavetti brought the guys in to get it, the alarms were all conveniently off.

But why? Why do all that? She made it almost too easy for Giavetti to get the stone. She gave him a place to hole up and experiment. She gave him cash and the means to get what he wanted, and used Imperial as a front to hide it all.

But if she wanted to help him, why not just give him the stone? And why set up an elaborate auction just to get him a book that was a forgery, anyway?

Because he's not stupid, and he wouldn't have fallen for it.

"She set him up," I say.

Gabriela looks at me. "What do you mean?"

"She set it up so that Giavetti would get the stone and the book and not think he was walking into a trap. She made him work to get them."

"I'm not following. I thought the book was a fake. Why would she do that?"

"Because she's still pissed off at him. It's a four-hundred-year-old grudge. She wants him to use the stone and the book. He'll think he's getting immortality."

"And instead it kills him," Gabriela says. "Like really kills him."

"She doesn't care about where Giavetti is," I say. "She cares about where the stone is. She *wants* Giavetti to get hold of it. If Giavetti figures out Frank has it, I'm fucked."

"He already knows where it is," she says.

I start to ask what she means and stop myself. Tonight's the night for understanding just how big a moron I am. Of course he knows.

Frank told him.

Chapter 25

Gabriela shoves her way into the passenger seat of my car before I can hit the lock. She makes a sour face.

"What the hell is that smell?" she asks. "Like something died in here."

"Me," I say. I haven't had a chance to really clean the car out too well.

"Ugh. Need to get you an air freshener." She pulls her seat belt on.

"You're not coming with me."

"Drop it," she says. "I've got a stake in this, too."

"I don't want you getting hurt."

She gets a weird look on her face for a second before it's replaced by the hardness I've started to expect.

"Don't worry," she says. "I've already made a deal with Darius. If I'm not around to help you, he'll try."

"That's not what I meant," I say.

"Just drive." I decide it would be more of a pain in the ass to kick her out at this point. I pull the car into the road and head for the freeway.

Frank's place is in a condo overlooking Echo Park. It's after midnight, but traffic's heavy. Backed up all the way to the freeway.

When we get there, we figure out why. I park a block away but close enough to see the paramedics, enough black-and-whites to make their own parade. Blue and red lights strobe off a sheet-covered gurney, dark stains soaking through.

Though I tell myself it could be something else, I know Giavetti's already been here. "We're too late," I say.

"No," she says, "we're not. Come on. We don't have a lot of time." She bolts out of the car. I follow her toward the crowd of gawkers gathered at the edges.

She's taking a bunch of fast, deep breaths. The way a swimmer does when he's about to go under.

"I hate this part," she says, grabbing my hand. Tight. "Don't let go."

The world goes the kind of flickering gray you see in silent movies. Skipping frames, stuttering lights. The crowd thins to a handful of people, all of them jerking along like bad animation.

"What just happened?"

The sounds of traffic, the chatter of the crowd, it's all gone. There's nothing but the sound of a wind I can't feel.

"Don't touch any of the ghosts," she says, pointing at the few remaining people. "And don't let go of me. It'll be okay." She grips my hand tighter for emphasis. I'm not sure which of us she's trying to reassure.

I catch a better look at a guy in a hoodie and low slung jeans as he skitters past me. The hoodie hides his face, but his eyes burn like they're on fire. Gun in his hand, a hole in his chest. Casting about like he's looking for something.

"They've all died," Gabriela says. "They don't last long out here. A few hours. A couple days. If they're around more than a week they're here for the long haul."

We make our way to the gurney, Gabriela shivering every few steps. "Problem?"

"No," she says. "All those cops you saw when we got here? They're still around. You can't see them, but you can walk through them. You can't feel it?"

I cast my hand around, searching. "Not a thing."

We duck under the sawhorses blocking the scene. With all the cops gone, the gurney looks barren and alone. The sheet covering it is bloody, stains coming up through the fabric.

Gabriela pulls the sheet down to show Frank, clawed and torn. Hard to tell just how badly he's messed up, his whole body is flickering in and out of focus. Safe to say he's missing a lot of meat.

Gabriela touches him lightly on the forehead. He snaps into focus, jerks on the gurney like he's touching a live wire. His eyes flutter open, blazing out of his face.

He holds my gaze a moment, and says, "I'm in hell, aren't I?"

"Good to see you, too."

He struggles to sit up, propping himself on one arm. The other's been chewed off at the shoulder, flaps of meat dangling down his side. He looks down at his ravaged chest, not quite sure what to make of the damage there.

"That's a big hole," he says.

"You're dead," Gabriela says.

"She's brilliant," he says to me. "Where'd you find her?"

"Skid Row."

"Figures."

I reach over to help him sit up, but Gabriela grabs my hand. "Don't touch him. I mean it."

Instead I say, "You know who did this?"

"Like you have to ask."

"We don't have time," Gabriela says. "Just answer his questions."

"Look, *chica*, I don't know who—" Frank starts, but Gabriela silences him with a wave of her hand. He stops like she's hit the pause button.

"I said answer his questions."

Neat trick. I try again: "Who did this?"

"Giavetti," he says, voice a monotone.

"What happened?"

"I was going to give him the stone. Had him come to my place. He had a dog, like a mastiff. It attacked me. I shot it, but it wouldn't go down."

"I don't get it. Why? What was he gonna give you for the rock?"

"He was going to bring my brother back to life."

He catches me with that one. I was expecting maybe some weird plan to have him get his guard down and then try to take him. But not this.

"Joe," Gabriela says, urgency in her voice. "We have to go."

I've been so focused on Frank I haven't been paying attention. The dead have been heading toward us for the last few minutes. They've surrounded us in a loose ring, and they're closing in. Not slow, just unfocused. Like they know we're here, but can't find us.

"What do they want?"

"Me," she says. "No more time."

I ignore her. "Where's Giavetti now?"

"I don't know," Frank says. "I was dead before he left."

The guy in the hoodie has gotten within an arm's length of me. I don't know what will happen if he touches me, but Gabriela doesn't give me a chance to find out.

The world snaps back into blinding focus, the murmur of the city a deafening roar. Cars, sirens, shocked paramedics.

Gabriela collapses against me, her face ashen. A cop comes toward us, reaching for his gun. And stops, eyes searching for us. The words on Gabriela's camouflage shirt glow bright and blue. She's got a grip on me like a vise. "Don't let go of me," she says and passes out.

———

"She knows not to do this," Darius says. We're down in the bar. I brought her here, and Darius told me to get her upstairs into a bed right away. Get her warmed up and keep her that way. Let her sleep. He gave me a candle to light by her bed. Thing stunk like a three-day-old corpse.

He didn't make any wisecracks, so I knew it was bad.

"I told her the last time not to do this again," he says.

"Is she going to be okay?"

"None of them touched her, right?"

"No. She touched one of them, though." I tell him about her reviving Frank.

"She should be fine, if she did it right. She'll be out for a while, though. That candle will help."

"Could what she did have killed her?"

"Could have?" he says. "Dead Man, it did. That's how it works. Stay too long and that's it. One of them touches you it tears away any life you've got left." He gives me a hard stare.

"She died to help you," he says, "and she almost didn't come back. I hope you appreciate that."

"She died to help her people," I say. "All her junkie vampires. Her disenfranchised undead. She wants the stone so she can keep Giavetti from using it. She didn't do this to help me."

"Damn. And I thought I was a cynic. What makes you think you're not one of her 'disenfranchised undead'? The hell do you think you are?"

"I'm not her people, Darius. I'm just a problem she doesn't need."

"Hmph. Dead Man, you don't know a goddamn thing."

Chapter 26

I wonder if I tore Samantha's heart out of her chest and ate it, would it kill her or just piss her off?

I know I'm stalling. Sitting here in the car a block from her building. I'm sure she knows I'm coming. But this time I doubt she wants to see me.

I check the Glock for the third time. Don't know why. Not like I'm going to shoot her. Probably wouldn't be any point, anyway.

I've stalled long enough. She knows where Giavetti is, and she'll tell me if I have to beat it out of her. I get out of the car and walk.

There's a different guard inside the foyer this time. He tries to step in front of me, but I ignore him.

"Can I help you, sir?" he says, putting one hand out and the other on the taser he's got clipped to his belt.

"No, I'm good, thanks." I punch the button on the elevator.

"Sir, I'm going to have to ask you to leave the premises."

"Or what? You're gonna shock me?" I'm making him nervous. The most he has to deal with on a regular night are homeless men pissing in the garden. I lurch out at him, waggle my fingers. Go, "Boo."

He shoves the taser into my throat.

The electricity runs through me, but it doesn't find much to hang on to. My eyelid twitches, but that's about it. From the look on his face, I'd say the guard's more shocked than I am.

I backhand him across the face, grab his wrist at the same time. There's a pop as his shoulder separates. He howls, but only for a second. The taser shuts him up pretty quick; a couple pops to the head and he won't be getting up any time soon.

I haul him to his feet, twitching and unconscious. We ride to the penthouse, me and this poor fucker who has no idea what he's gotten himself into.

When the doors open, I toss him across the floor to Samantha's waiting feet.

She glances at him, takes a sip of her martini. "Feel better?"

"A little."

"I heard about Neumann," she says. "And I know your friend is awake."

"You know what he told us?"

She holds a moment, assessing. "Interesting. Couple of days ago I wouldn't have figured you two to be an 'us.' What's the lucky lady's name again?"

I ignore her. "I know about Imperial Enterprises, the auction, the house. I don't know how you got the stone in the first place, but that doesn't really matter, does it?"

"Then why are you here? Just to tell me about everything I've done?"

Why am I here? I kept telling myself that I wanted her to tell me where Giavetti had holed up. But do I really?

Or do I want her to deny all of it?

"I know you kept Carl from talking," I say. "How come? Why didn't you just kill him?"

"Dear god, why would I do that? I'm not cruel," she says.

No, but she is crazy. I consider telling her about all the people Giavetti's killed trying to get the stone or use it properly. But I don't think it would matter. She's too far gone for that.

"It's like that joke about the two guys walking in the woods when they run into a bear," she says. "And one of them starts putting on track shoes. And he says to his friend, 'I don't have to outrun the bear, I just have to outrun you.' Joe, the truth was going to come out eventually. I just needed to make sure Sandro didn't catch on until it was too late."

"So, what's gonna happen when Giavetti uses the rock and the book of fake instructions?"

A psychotic smile creeps onto her face. "It'll kill him. Slowly. The meat's going to fall from his bones. His eyes are going to ooze out of their sockets. And he's going to get to feel every excruciating moment."

And I thought I had it bad. "Why?" I say. "It's been four hundred years, for chrissake."

She laughs. It's a bitter sound, ripping through the air. Centuries of resentment, anger, and god knows what else, all in that driving cackle. You can feel her age in it. She cuts it off, throwing her martini to shatter against the wall as punctuation.

"Can you really be that stupid?" she says. The anger was coming off her in waves. "Why do you think? He murdered me, Joe. He drove a knife in my chest and stuck me in the ground. For two fucking weeks."

She tries to compose herself, hands like claws raking over her face, bunching into fists. But it's too much.

"And he kept murdering me. Him and every other jackal out there. Live long enough, every horror a human being can do to another is going to happen to you."

"I—"

"No. Shut up. You don't get it. Have you any idea how many times I've been stabbed? Raped? Burned alive? You don't know what it's like. I was dipped in acid over the course of a month before it killed me. I've had the skin flayed from my bones. You have no fucking idea what I've been through. What he's put me through. He left me in that goddamn box for two goddamn weeks, and that was cake. And nothing I could ever do to him was half as bad as what he did to me. I killed him. And I kept killing him. Over and over again, but he kept coming back. Like a fucking cockroach. He. Keeps. Coming. BACK."

Her breath hitches, tears stream down her cheeks. I should do something, say something, but I don't know what. Hug her? Shoot her? She doesn't give me the chance to make a decision.

"So, you want to know why I'm killing him?" she asks. "Because this time I'm going to make it stick."

Her face is twisted with all the years of grief, and horror, and nightmare that she's lived through. Pouring it all into her hatred of Giavetti.

And just as quickly, it's gone. Sweet, beautiful Samantha again. She sniffles, gives me a smile. Wipes the tears from her cheeks. She crosses over to the bar, pours gin into a new glass. Slams it back.

"I give a fuck about Giavetti," I say. But I care about her. I shouldn't. She's the one got me here. She's bugfuck crazy, but god help me I do. But, like her, I've got other priorities. "You know what's going to happen to me, don't you?"

She nods, looks me in the eyes. "Joe," she says. "You're so sweet. And so young. And I really care about you." Sincerity dripping over every word. "But there isn't anything I can do. It's over. Sandro's got the stone now. Not as quickly as I'd planned it, and with more collateral damage than I'd intended, but he's got it, and that's all that matters. I know you won't believe me, but this is true. I'm really sorry you're going to die."

"No," I say. That's not going to happen. "You're gonna tell me where he is." I draw the Glock, rack the slide. She laughs at me.

"If you kill me, you'll never know. I don't heal like you. For me it's slow. I'll be dead at least a day and by that time Sandro will be gone, you'll be gone, and I'll be heading down to a nice little villa I have down in Cabo."

"I can still hurt you."

"You're not listening to me. I've been hurt before. By professionals. Men and women who knew what they were doing. And they're all dead now. All I have to do is wait it out."

"I can be pretty persuasive." She's right, though. If I shoot her, she dies. And by the time she comes back it'll all be over. And nothing I can do to her will be half as bad as what she's already lived through.

"I know you can," she says. "The other night I almost— Let's say I could think of worse things to do than spend a couple hundred years hanging out with you. If you'd stayed, we might not be having this conversation."

I should have figured what she was really doing when she went to the bar, but when she whips the snub-nose .38 from behind a bottle I'm surprised.

Now it's my turn to laugh. "Oh, come on. What the hell is that gonna do?" I put my hands in the air. "Go ahead. Put holes in me."

In the distance I can hear sirens. Loud and getting close.

"I had the guard call the police while you were still downstairs," she says. "I pay him enough to remember the story. Even after what you've done to him."

Fuck. The last thing I need. "Getting me locked up? That's cheating."

She throws me a dismissive wave. "Oh, you'll walk away from this," she says. "I have faith. Besides, as far as the police are concerned you're a short, overweight Asian man with a Mohawk. No, I just needed a little insurance so you won't walk off and try to take me with you. I can't take the chance you might convince me to tell you where he is." Her face softens with something that might be sorrow.

"Torture wouldn't do it," she says, "but that look on your face. Flash those eyes at me a few times, and I'd tell you anything. I so didn't want to do this to you. If nothing else, please believe that."

She shoves the barrels under her chin and pulls the trigger.

Chapter 27

The blast is deafening. Her body jerks as the bullet blows through the top of her head. Everything above her nose shatters like a birthday piñata, streamers of blood showering the ceiling.

I run to her. I grab her as she collapses. Blood pumping from a heart that hasn't figured out its job is over.

Somewhere, in the back of my mind, I know this is temporary. I know she'll be fine, and that this is only a quick escape route. But I'm holding her, shaking her, yelling at her just the same. She was right, I realize; I couldn't have hurt her.

Hadn't realized how much she could hurt me, though.

A groan behind me pulls me back to the real world. The guard twitches, eyes fluttering. I don't give him the chance to wake up. I kick him in the head to keep him out. I can only hope he's as professional as Samantha thinks. I don't want Santa Monica's finest looking for me.

I can hear the cops' footsteps on the stairs, see the elevator's slow crawl upward.

I run to a back window overlooking the alley below. This isn't such a bad idea. Right? Maybe it won't suck as much as I think it will. Besides, it's not like I've never jumped out a window before. Just not from eight stories up.

Cops are kicking the door in. I heave myself out of the window, get a second to regret doing it before I clip the roof of a Volvo. Both legs shatter. I bounce off it, scraping my face across the pavement. Bone crunches, skin shreds. I drag myself behind a Dumpster, wait a moment for my legs to rearrange themselves enough that I can hobble off.

I give Samantha's apartment one final look. Wonder if I'll see her again. And what will happen when I do.

———

"You all right?" Gabriela leans against the doorway of one of the Edge-wood's rooms. She's got hangover eyes, the slouch of the terminally ex-hausted.

"Me? Darius said you were gonna be out cold all night."

She waves the idea away. "What does he know?" she says. "He's just a demon. And you're avoiding the question."

I've showered, changed into a leftover set of clothes from one of her vampires.

Gabriela must be feeling sorry for me. I'm on my second cigarette, and she hasn't tried to put it out.

"Meh. I'm okay. Mostly just feeling stupid."

I fill her in on what happened at Samantha's. She makes the appro-priate sympathetic noises at the right moments. She's good. Power aside, I can see why people flock to her.

"You trusted her, didn't you?" she asks.

"Doesn't happen often. Don't think it'll happen again anytime soon."

"Trust isn't so bad, you know. I trusted you. You came through for me."

"Hey, you're still my best bet in all this. Besides, you'd have been fine."

She crosses the threshold, sits next to me on the bed. "No, I wouldn't have. You gave me an anchor. Something to come back to. Land of the dead's not a fun place to get stuck."

She says to the guy with no pulse.

"Wasn't me bringing you back."

She pauses a moment, a word on her lips. Whatever it was, she changes her mind. "Yeah, I suppose you're right," she says. She slaps my thigh, stands up. "But enough of this emo bullshit. We need to find that rock."

"I'm out of ideas. My only lead's leaking in the back of a morgue wagon right about now. I appreciate all this, really, but the rock's gone. Pretty soon Giavetti's going to do his thing, and it'll all be over. I'll be out of your hair. Better I just go find a hole to wait it out in."

I've been thinking about packing it in since I got back. Really, what's the point? Giavetti uses that thing, and I'm going to flake away like government cheese.

"Jesus, you're a pussy," she says. "You're this goddamn close, and you want to give up?"

"You know where Giavetti's at? I'm tapped. Better he just use the damn thing. Solve all my problems. This point, I just want it over."

"I don't know where he is, but I know someone who does."

———

I don't know why we didn't think of this sooner. Probably because neither one of us wanted to pay the price.

"I'm beginning to think it's time to renegotiate," Darius says, wiping down the bar with a cloth. I'm still not clear on whether any of this is real, but the drinks are good, so I guess it doesn't really matter.

"Oh come on," Gabriela says. "We've got a contract."

"That either one of us can break at any time," he says. He flexes his enormous shoulders. "And I'm feelin' a mite cooped up of late."

"I don't know why we're doing this," I say. "We've been over this before. He can't find the rock. Even if he could, he can't tell us where it is."

"Don't go presupposing for me, Dead Man," Darius says. "I know things you can't even imagine."

"Yeah, and it means fuck all to me right now. Do you know where it is or not?" According to Gabriela, since Samantha died the spell keeping the stone hidden should have dissolved with her. Even when she comes back from the dead, anything that she's done should still be gone. So now Darius should be able to pinpoint it.

"Of course, I do. But that's privileged information. We're not betting on the ponies, here. You want the whereabouts of the stone, it's going to require a special price."

"What is it?" Gabriela asks.

"I want a night with you, sweet thing," he says. He chucks her gently on the chin. His smile is all teeth.

Gabriela, already a little pasty faced, goes a shade whiter. "What about the rest of our contract?" she asks. "If you're renegotiating here, is that your new asking price for everything?"

He thinks a moment. "No. Same terms for the rest."

"Not to break up a budding romance," I say, "but there's still the problem of actually telling us."

"Oh, like you didn't figure it out the last time. I'll just make it easier on ya." He puts up three fingers. "Scout's promise."

Gabriela seems to be seriously considering it. "Deal," she says finally, putting out her hand. "When my next question is about the location of the rock, and you answer it, you have me for one night. Nothing rough. Nothing painful. All other questions are covered by the same terms."

"Whoa. I don't think so," I say. Gabriela puts her other hand up to stop me.

"Not your decision," Darius says. I swear he's drooling.

"Do we have a deal, then?"

Darius' hand swallows hers, and he pumps it like he's pulling water from a well. There's a sound just beyond my hearing. Like a pop, only not. Like a sound a sound makes when it's not there.

"Don't worry," he says to me with a wink, "I'll be gentle. Now, ask away."

"Where is Giavetti holding his ritual?" Gabriela says.

Darius blinks at her.

"You bitch," he says, though there's an admiring tone in his voice.

"Okay, what just happened?" I ask.

"Never said I wanted to know where the stone was," she says. "My next question wasn't about the stone. And he has to follow the rules. So give. Where is he?"

He lets loose with a belly laugh that shakes the room. "See," he says to me, "this is why I like her. Reminds me of a girl I knew in Persia way back when."

He clears his throat, cracks his neck. His eyes roll back in his head. Really making a show of it. "He's in the junkyard," he says, his voice a carny fortune-teller's.

"Junkyard?" Gabriela asks. "What junkyard?"

"Mackay Salvage," I say. Jesus. Samantha really went to town on this one. Got Giavetti the stone, got him the book, even got him a place to fuck himself in. "It's close. Next to the river." I give her a rundown on the place, how I found it.

"Okay," she says. "So we head over and—" The room shudders like it's been hit by a city bus.

My guts twist with it, and fire shoots down my arms. Pain's something I'd got used to not feeling, and the sudden shock of it sends me to my knees. It passes with the same sudden shock it came with.

"The hell was that?"

"Brownout," she says, helping me stand. "He's started."

"Brownout?"

"The stone's tapping into the local reservoirs," Darius says. He's not looking too comfortable with all this. "Drawing power. A lot of it. You have to go. Now."

I'm getting that same sinking feeling I've gotten when I'm starting to rot. Only I don't have the same hunger. I look at my hands. They're starting to sink in on themselves. Going gray. Dark blotches are fading up through the skin.

The bar shudders again, and that blast of pain staggers me. Gabriela pulls me hard toward the door.

Darius is sweating. "Another shake up like that and I'm not sure I can keep my door open," Darius says. He's got a calm veneer, but something in his voice has me worried.

"This place isn't a place," Gabriela says to my questioning look. She's shoving me along, and I'm having trouble keeping up. "It exists independent of the local pool, but the door doesn't. He draws on that power to keep it open to the hotel. The power drops too much, and the door to the hotel shuts. Then we're stuck."

"And if it goes away completely?" My voice is cracked and hoarse, like it's got holes in it.

"The bar disappears," Darius says. "Oh, it's still here, but it won't look like this. The surroundings won't be quite so . . . pleasant."

"What about you?" I ask him.

"I'll be fine. This place is all for your benefit, not mine. Go on. Git."

The bar patrons, figments of Darius' overactive imagination, start to snap out of existence. A dancer goes. Then another. Then whole swaths of them. The music disappears instrument by instrument as phantom jazz musicians disintegrate on stage. It's like watching popcorn in reverse. The walls shimmer, get indistinct.

We run to the door. Halfway there my left leg goes numb. I drag it the rest of the way. Gabriela yanks the door open. The hotel lobby's on the other side, but it's flickering like a bad print of a Chaplin film.

"Fuck," she says.

"That's bad?"

"Very." You can almost smell the gears turning in her head, weighing odds, looking for options. A weird calm settles over her.

"If I go through when it flickers out," she says, "I won't be coming through alive." The flickering is getting worse, the dark spaces noticeably longer.

"We're stuck?" A flake of skin drifts lazily off my forehead to the floor.

"We's too many people," she says. "You're already dead."

"No. You're not staying here. You can't. There's got to be another way out of here. Darius said—"

"Darius is oversimplifying. No, it won't be pleasant, but it won't kill me to be here when the lights go out."

"Do you know that for sure? What happens when this place goes dark?"

She looks back at Darius. He's washing shot glasses. Whistling to himself. Trying to be calm. He's not fooling anyone. The glasses pop out of existence as soon as he puts them down.

"No," she says. "But I do know that I'll die if I go through now." She's trying hard to maintain, but I can see the fear in her eyes.

"If I get Giavetti before all the power's gone—"

"Then the bar, the door, all of it, should come back. Hopefully, I'll come back with it."

"I'll stop him. I'll get you out of here."

"I know. I'd kiss you for good luck, but you're going a little green."

"That happens."

"I won't hold it against you. Now go. Before I kick you through."

There's no way to time it, so I just step through. There's a roar in my ears, a sense of cold and hot at the same time. My vision goes black.

When I can see again, I'm through. My clothes are smoking a little. The hotel lobby's just as it was. I turn back to the door.

But it's already gone.

Chapter 28

Driving to the junkyard is a challenge. I'm going fast. Faster than before. The skin on my hands has split, spilling thick blood across the steering wheel. The tendons in my left ankle snap halfway there, and I have to shift gears with a flopping foot that might as well be a stump.

If my nose hadn't already shriveled into my face I'd probably mind the smell. As it is, I can barely stand catching a hint of my reflection in the rearview mirror.

Day one I should have gotten myself embalmed.

As I cut through downtown toward the river, I can see I'm not the only one hurting.

There's a minor riot going on, and the cops are out in force. I can't help but think it's Gabriela's homeless vampires going apeshit. The schizophrenic normals can't be helping. I can't tell who's who.

To everyone else it probably looks like a lot of junkies in Skid Row got the same bad batch of heroin. But in one of the scattered crowds I think I recognize the woman Gabriela brought in the other day to pay Darius. She's screaming, shrieking like Ethel Merman with her pubes on fire. Doing her part to add to the general noise and chaos. She's got three cops on her. Tosses them into a street lamp like she's shrugging off a sheet.

I pass by just as they start in on her with the tasers. I can't do anything for her.

I turn the radio to a news station. This isn't the only place shit's happening. The news reports have already started. The city's gone bugfuck, and nobody knew it was coming.

If Gabriela and Darius are right, it will be over soon, one way or another.

It starts to rain about a block later. We're in the middle of a drought. Nothing for six months and now this. It starts as the kind of spatter that you can call rain only because it's damp and falling from the sky.

But it gets worse fast. It's slow going as months of road oil lift up, makes the streets slick. If nothing else gets on the news tonight, this will. We do rain like some people do rivers of blood. I can't think of a better sign of an L.A. apocalypse than water from the sky.

By the time I pull up to Mackay Salvage, sheets of it are pouring down on the city. This isn't an L.A. rain. This is a winter in Seattle rain.

I pull into the gravel lot, tires sloshing through new puddles. It's empty but for three cars: a beat up F-150, a Corolla, and a Mercedes that looks like it's just off the showroom floor.

Danny's car. Interesting. I wonder if he's in the trunk.

There's another wave of gut twisting. They're coming more frequently now, and the skin on my right pinky sloughs off to bone. If I don't do something soon, there's not going to be any of me left.

I shuffle inside, left foot dragging behind, Glock held tight in my hand. It's getting harder to hold as I lose skin and muscle.

I wend my way through stacks of dead cars, gutted engines, listening, trying to hear for a sign of Giavetti. It's tough. My right ear has gone completely deaf, and I can barely see through the rain and my tunnel vision. Everything looks like it's seen through a fish-eye lens.

There's a growl behind me. I spin toward it, almost lose my balance. One hand on a fender, the other on my pistol. Giavetti's mastiff stares at me.

The thing is huge. Rain slicks across its back, pooling in its jaws. It's the size of a fucking horse. Got teeth you could shred a car with.

But it's not the dog that grabs my attention.

"That you, Joe?" Danny asks. Porkpie hat pushed back onto his bald head, water soaking into his jacket. He doesn't look scared. Nervous, yeah, but not like he should with that dog towering over him. He shines a flashlight over me, his brain finally getting what his eyes are telling it. The horror on his face thick as clown makeup.

"Yeah, it's me." My voice comes through like it's run through a cheese grater. I wonder how much longer I'll be able to talk. "What are you doing here, Danny?"

He should be gone. Dead or skipped town, but not here with Giavetti's mastiff acting like he's its babysitter.

"He made me a deal." He sounds dubious. "He's going to—"

"Make you live forever?" I finish. "I know about his deals. Look at me. This is what you'll get. Didn't figure you for stupid. Thought you'd be smart enough to run to Mexico, Giavetti on your ass and all. That story on the phone just bullshit?"

"No," he says, voice wavering. "He really did tear Bruno's face off. But he caught me outside the hospital. Told me about the stone, what it could do. What it did to you." His voice trails off.

I spread my arms out, limp in a slow circle so he can get a good look. "Pretty cool, huh? The ladies'll fuckin' flock to you with a look like this, yeah? Come on, Danny, don't buy into the bullshit. Look at me. This is what he's offering. This is his idea of immortality."

Danny's shaking his head. "He told me about you. What happened to you. Said he screwed things up. Figured it out this time. Told me how you stabbed him in the back and ripped him off. I helped him get the stone back. I'm gonna live forever."

I laugh. A wet, grinding cough. Bad brakes on a steep hill. "Come on. Like you don't know a con when you see it. He needs you for something else. Otherwise, once he had the stone, he'd have just thrown you away."

"Don't listen to him, kid," Giavetti says, stepping from behind a stack of trashed cars. "Look at him. He's just bitter."

But Danny's wondering. I can see it in his eyes. He's not buying it. Narcissistic fuck. A little slow, but he's not stupid. You can almost hear the gears grinding inside his head.

Giavetti notices it, too. He steps up behind him, slaps a friendly hand on his shoulder. "I keep my word," he says. "You'll live forever."

He shoves a wicked looking blade through Danny's back, punching it out through his chest. Danny lurches, tries to steady himself, grab at the blade.

"Kids these days," Giavetti says. He yanks the blade free, wipes the blood on Danny's rain-soaked jacket. Danny slides to the ground. Still alive but probably not for long.

"Not sure which one of you pisses me off more," I say. "You for being such a dick, or him for being such an idiot."

"Hey, I gave him my word. He'll live forever. More or less. I mean, you know, in me." He crouches down to Danny. "Sorry kid. I meant to tell you. See, I'm old. Look at me. But you, you're nice and young and, well, I could use some of that youth, you know? So, I'll be taking yours. No hard feelings?"

Danny makes a halfhearted swipe at Giavetti and starts a gurgling scream. Giavetti kicks him to shut him up.

"This won't work," I say.

"Why? Because Sam's book is bullshit?" I'm not sure if I've got enough of a face left to show my surprise, but he catches it, anyway. "What, you thought I didn't know about that? Come on. Bitch has been trying to kill me for half a millennium. You think I'm going to trust her now? No, this one's going to stick."

He starts to walk away, ignoring me like I'm just some insignificant nuisance. Yeah, well, this nuisance has a big fucking gun.

I take a shot, but my aim is so off it punches a hole in a radiator a good ten feet above his head instead.

The dog springs, ready to jump, but Giavetti stays it with his hand.

"Jesus, you just don't give up, do you? I don't have time for this crap." He pulls the stone out of his pocket. It's throwing out a glow like it's on fire. It's hard to see Giavetti past its brilliance. I tear my eyes away from it, shift my aim.

But I can't pull the trigger. My arm locks up. Pulling against it just makes it shake like I've got chronic Parkinson's.

Giavetti plucks the gun out of my hand. With a quick slide he dismantles it, drops the pieces on the ground in front of me.

"Doesn't it suck," he says, "to have salvation just out of reach?" He turns away to leave. "Killer," he says to the dog. "Sic him."

The mastiff charges. I can't move. It grabs me in its jaws like a chew toy and tosses me into a stack of Volvos. My gun clatters to the ground. I hear bones crunch. My left arm snaps at the shoulder.

And this time it hurts.

Giavetti watches the dog bounce me around a couple of times before he decides to leave his pet to play with its food. If he says anything, I can't hear him past the rain and the ringing in my head. Besides, I think my ears have been torn off.

The dog tosses me like a Frisbee. I carom off stacks of old cars, busted trucks. The pain's so intense I don't really much feel it anymore.

It would be nice if I could pass out, but the best I can hope for is the dog finally crunches on my skull and makes it all stop.

I come crashing down into the open top of a car compactor, the one I dropped the guards into the other night. My already useless left leg snaps into a pretzel. Without thinking I twitch my remaining hand and grab the edge before falling in. It barely holds.

But it does. Whatever Giavetti did to me is wearing off. I can sort of jerk my body up, grab the edge, inch my way up with numb fingers. I feel like I'm full of novocaine for all the control I've got, but with some creative twitching I get myself up and over the lip.

Not that it helps much. I'm lying on a thin ledge of machinery, the ground fifteen feet below me on one side, the yawning gap of the compactor on the other. I'd opt for the ground, but the mastiff's growl below me doesn't make that a particularly attractive option.

There's a blur of black as it leaps to a high ledge to look down at me. It stands on a teetering tower of Detroit's finest. One jump and a quick snap of its jaws, and it should be over. If I'm lucky.

But I'm not done just yet. It springs from its high perch and with what little coordination I've got left, I roll myself off the ledge to the gravel below.

The mastiff hits the compactor with a thud that would put a train wreck to shame. It lets out a bellow, tries to scramble out. But there's not much for it to grab. Enough time and it will probably find a way.

Better I not give it any. I drag myself over to the controls, strength slowly returning to my shattered limbs. It's just like what I did the other night. Only with more meat.

I shove my whole weight against the ON button and the machine jerks to life.

The grinding of metal gives way to the shriek of Giavetti's demon dog as the compactor folds in on itself. Its howling turns to screams, high-pitched squeals that should never come out of a thing that big.

In a few moments there's no sound but the machinery grinding it into paste.

I pull myself away, a trail of meat and shattered bone behind me. Losing more and more of myself at every inch. I can't remember where my legs went.

Seconds crawl by. Feels like hours, days. I can't tell. Every second's turned into a meaningless eternity. They pile up on each other. Waves against sand, the slow grind of inevitability. At some point they all catch up with each other and time comes crashing back in on me.

It's still night. The moon is still shining down, a thin white crescent in the dank blue of a darkened sky.

I'm not gone. I'm mostly bone held together by gristle. I'm missing an arm, both legs, most of my face. But I'm not gone. Through rotting holes, I can see the tendons in the hand I have left.

I can feel the stone nearby. Like that one girl you knew you'd give everything for. As soon as she walked into the room, you knew it. The one you swore you'd crawl on hands and knees over broken glass for.

So I crawl.

It takes a thousand forevers. Every foot is a mile.

The hallways of burned-out husks and crushed junkers opens into a field of twisted metal. Cars piled high like trees. Danny hangs upside down, strung from the fender of a Studebaker, one leg suspended, the other crossed over behind it like an inverted 4. I think he's still alive. But he won't be for long.

I watch, fascinated. Danny gets older by the second. Fingernails grow long, skin warps and wrinkles. He curls in on himself as his spine shrinks. Every second of his youth is draining away.

Giavetti lies underneath him on the roof of a desiccated Volvo, spread-eagled. What's left of Danny's blood drips down onto him. Onto the stone resting on his forehead.

And with each drop Giavetti is getting younger.

The stone's brilliance catches me for a moment. I can take it. Just crawl up, and it's mine. Let it heal me, take me away from this horror show I've turned into. I start to lurch forward, catch myself in a lucid moment that's becoming less frequent as the seconds tick by.

If I take it, Giavetti will just come back for it, and I'm back at square one. I'm nothing but sticks held together by shreds of skin now. I've left a trail of intestines and blood across the gravel like some demon slug. Skin nothing but shredded paste. My mind is unraveling like a cheap sweater.

I remember what Darius said about killing Giavetti. Maybe taking the stone just won't be enough.

I pull a chunk of twisted metal from the ground. It's long and sharp and makes a perfect shiv. Crawl onto the Volvo, look at Danny hanging there. A slice in his throat like a new, bloody mouth stares at me, face slick with rain and his own draining blood. We look at each other. I can see a plea to kill him in his eyes. In due time, kid. I got priorities.

I climb over Giavetti, press the shiv against his throat. I'd say something witty, but my tongue fell off a while ago.

I close my eyes, pray to whatever sick twisted fuck there might be in heaven that this works, and ram the shiv through him as I pull the stone off his forehead.

The effect is immediate. The stone flashes bright and purple, and I can feel my skin fill in, new bones grow, muscles wrap themselves together like cables. My rotted flesh sloughs off to be washed away by the rain.

Beneath me Giavetti screams and thrashes around. I stab and keep stabbing. Slicing jagged holes through him. He reaches up to ward me off, but as I get stronger he gets weaker.

Finally, I bring the shiv down into his chest, tear through the sternum. My hands dig into the hole, make it wider. Yank flesh and bone aside.

I bend my face down to the shredded hole in his chest and lose myself in the feast.

Chapter 29

I roll over in a pool of dripping gore, stare at the sun burning in a crystal blue sky. Most beautiful sunrise I've ever seen. The stone is heavy in my hand, pulsing.

I don't know how long I've been out. Long enough to grow everything back. Legs, hand—I check the inside of my mouth. Yep, even tongue. I take an experimental breath, pull air into my lungs, waiting for that rush that tells me everything's fine, that this was all some kind of bad dream.

But it's just like inflating a balloon. I'm still dead.

I pull myself up. My clothes are shredded rags, my pants in particular. They look like bad cutoffs from the seventies. Parts of me are covered in thick slime, a holdover, it seems, from my rotting spell the night before. I stink like a fucking slaughterhouse in summer.

Where Giavetti should be, splayed out on the roof of the Volvo beneath me, there are just bones and scraps of meat. And I thought I went to town on Neumann. There's hardly anything left.

But it might still be enough. I gather up the bones and put them into an empty oil drum. Pour gasoline over them. Light them on fire. Let them cook.

I find some old work overalls in the junkyard's office and put them on in place of my torn up clothes. They're not great, but they're better than walking around in blood-soaked Daisy Dukes.

I cut Danny down. His wizened body is light as a child's. Poor bastard. I lay him down on the ground and go out front to bring in his car. Park it far in the back and pull the plates. Nobody will find it. No one will come looking.

Danny's featherweight corpse goes into the car compactor, a couple hundred pounds of scrap on top of him. It grinds him into paste.

Giavetti's charred bones get the same treatment, but only after I've broken them into as many small chunks as I can.

It takes a while. I run the compactor half a dozen times, adding more scrap each time. Whatever's left of Giavetti is sandwiched between broken headlights, radiator grills. I'd piss in there, if I could.

If that doesn't keep him dead, I don't know what will.

———

The drive to downtown is short. No one's on the road. It's nine in the morning, and the freeways should be packed. Something monumental happened last night, and it's almost as though the city knows it. The storm has passed. It's a fragile feeling. If you look at it too hard, it will pop like a soap bubble. I wonder how many people actually felt it, or even knew what it was.

I pull off the freeway and have to double back through side streets to get to Gabriela's place. The police have set up a webwork of crime scene tape, official looking sawhorses.

The radio paints a scene of intense, if short-lived, insanity last night. The official body count's still coming in, but it seems there were riots from Pasadena to San Pedro. Looting, arson, murder.

There's a story about some guys in gorilla suits running rampant through Griffith Park and killing the horses at the equestrian center. Another of a mob of homeless in Santa Monica killing half a dozen people on the Promenade and trying to eat them.

And then it all just stopped.

Not sure how I feel about that. I'm the one that did it. Does that make me a hero? Did I save the day? I decide I'm not the hero type and shut off the radio.

At Gabriela's hotel the bar is back. The red leather door in the wall just as out of place as it was before.

"Welcome back, Dead Man," Darius says as I step inside. He's got a tall Bloody Mary sitting on the bar in front of him, a lone celery stalk in the glass. "Slew the dragon, saved the fair maiden. You deserve a celebratory drink."

The band is playing some Glenn Miller tune. His phantom dancers are spinning each other slowly across the floor.

"What is it?" It doesn't smell quite like a Bloody Mary.

"Mostly V-8," Darius says. "Some tabasco. Some pepper. Other stuff."

Other stuff. "That's what worries me."

Darius laughs. "This is a gift. Cadaver hearts from unclaimed bodies. Gabriela knows a boy down at USC Medical. Grabs them before they get cremated. She'd hoped to get this stuff to you earlier, but the boy couldn't deliver until today. So drink up. It'll cure what ails ya."

I look at it. Think about it.

"Where is she, anyway?" I assumed she made it out all right or the guy at the front desk would have said something.

"Out tending to her flock. Lots of folk hurting out there this morning. Like suffering from the mother of all hangovers. She's making sure things are okay. So, whatta ya say? Partake of the kindness of the *Bruja?*"

"No," I say. "I didn't keep my end of the bargain. She only owes me this if I deliver the stone. I haven't delivered the stone."

"Ah," Darius says. "You know, bargains are funny things. You have to look at the wording. For example, she offered to find a way to keep you from rotting that didn't involve eating human hearts." He points to the drink. "That, my friend, is made out of human hearts. She didn't keep her end of the bargain, either."

"Of course, it's not like you need it." He reaches over and taps me on the chest with a wink.

I learned the hard way that a safe isn't very safe. Before I left the junkyard I tore a hole into my chest with a chunk of metal and shoved the stone up behind my sternum. It's sitting there nice and comfortable, and I've felt better with it there than I've felt the entire time I've been dead.

"Maybe you and I ought to talk about this," I say.

"Maybe we should. You know, that thing there's not exactly hidden. But at the same time, only some of us can actually see it. So, I have a proposition for you. Interested?"

"I'm all ears."

"I don't talk about your, ah, inside jewelry. But one of these days, I just might want to. And when that day comes, well, the only thing that'll keep my fool mouth shut is an incentive. Like, maybe a favor. Are you following me, Dead Man?"

"I'm following you. You say nothing. Tell no one. Don't even fucking hint that it's there. Ever. And you get one favor. That about the gist of it?"

"Oh, that's it exactly. Do we have a deal?" He puts out his meaty paw.

What's the big deal? Really? I don't want anyone knowing I've got this thing on me, not even Gabriela. It'd just cause problems I don't need.

And I do a job for Darius. I do jobs all the time.

"Deal." We shake on it and there's that weird non-pop sound in my ears that seals it.

"You might want to drink the drink, anyway. Looks less conspicuous that way. And I wouldn't want to tell our young miss that you didn't. She might get suspicious."

Good point. I down the drink. It's not bad.

Darius hands me a napkin. "You got a blood mustache," he says. I wipe my face.

"Thanks. I think."

A couple of Darius' phantom patrons cozy to the bar, order sidecars.

"Friendly advice," Darius says, shaking up nonexistent cocktails for nonexistent customers. "Get to know your new people."

"My people?"

"You know who I'm talking about. This here's a community, like it or not. It's bloodier than most, but nothing you shouldn't be able to handle. Things are different now. You got yourself some breathing room. Take in this brand new world. See what you can do with it."

"What's that friendly advice gonna cost me?"

"Friendly means free. Take it when it's offered. Doesn't happen often. Besides, I've taken a shine to you, Dead Man. I'd like to see you around. And Gabriela could use a hand. Coked-up vampires and sketchy gangbangers don't make for the most stable support system for a young lady."

Maybe he's right. I've jumped down the rabbit hole and, for the moment at least, Wonderland's not trying to kill me. Best I get the hang of it before it gets me.

"What about you?" I ask. "You work for her. What does she need me for?"

He laughs. "Oh, you don't get how this works, do you? No, no, no. I work for myself. I'm here because I like it here. It's nice and cozy. And the *Bruja*'s not the only game in town. No, I have my iron in a lot of fires. Never know which way the day will take you."

He reaches under the bar, pulls out a small envelope. My name is written on the front in a flowing script that looks disturbingly familiar. "Speaking of which," he says, "this is from a mutual acquaintance."

He slides the envelope over to me. I open it and pull out a note that reads, "I couldn't have done it without you. Love, Sam."

I stare at the note. There's a faint scent of perfume on it. The same scent she was wearing last night when she shot herself.

"When did you get this?"

"Oh, 'when' is such a subjective idea. Why be so linear about things?"

"Okay, *how* did you get this?" I thought I'd had it all figured out. Samantha dead, Giavetti gone. Now I don't know who's playing who.

Darius slides a scotch neat in front of me. "Have another drink, Dead Man," and gives me an inscrutable smile. "Enjoy it. You've earned it."